A Quarter Life Crisis

A Quarter Life Crisis

ISBN: 978-1-4716-7524-9

For Craig, Janine, Riada and Belle

Thanks to

Riada McCredie, who has been the most wonderfully supportive person throughout this whole process.

Sophie Lambert, who helped me to focus on what was important, her help was invaluable.

Gary Cocker, Gabriel Neil, Jamie Maxwell, Shala Hosein, Sian Cook and Catherine Macnab for all of their help, guidance and often contradictory advice. I've tried to take the best of it onboard.

Michael Selvadurai for his handy cover work and his feelings about Scrabble.

Finally, Janine Ewen and Craig Kelly. Without them there wouldn't be a book at all.

Peace and love

Andrew

Chapter 1

"I think that we should go on a break."

These were the words that began my quarter life crisis. They weren't even good words; the short sentence itself contained two different lies. When I had said "go on a break" what I really meant was "break up", and when I had said "I think that we should" then what I had really meant was "I want to". The speech that I had written in my head was far better; it was eloquent, sympathetic, sensitive and compassionate, it was even slightly witty. But it was worthless. As soon as I opened my mouth it all fell apart. I lost my place, I choked on my words, and I was left sounding feeble and heartless. After a short concentrated silence I tried to explain myself, but none of the things that I was saying mattered anymore. By the time that I had eventually managed to splutter anything out the damage had already been done.

***

The next few days were really hard, and they still play out in my head like some kind of fast paced, confusing cinematic montage rather than a full-blown experience. Even when I think about them now I can see everything being presented through multiple 'camera angles'. I can envisage myself looking chiselled and gray while she looks glamorous and entrapped in despair by what I had just done. I can imagine long drawn out looks of love and lore as we contemplated our individual and collective futures to an emotionally-charged, power chord layered, Bon Jovi soundtrack.

I really should have been better prepared for the uncomfortable aftermath. With hindsight I should have plotted like a heart-breaking Machiavelli and packed my bags before I had even said anything. If I had been more calculating then I could have already sorted out how I was going to tell her and where I was going to go afterwards. During the days that lead up to our irreversible conversation I hadn't been laying down any of the groundwork for the fallout. Instead I had been staying late at the office or hanging around with my friend Steven at the all night coffee shop until I thought that she would be in bed, that way I could delay the inevitable for a few days longer.

On the first night after our 'break' I slept on the couch, which was unbelievably uncomfortable, although it was even worse when I saw her in the hallway the next morning. It was a totally unsustainable situation as we kept desperately trying to stay out of each other's way in what was only a one bedroom flat. On the second night two of her friends visited and because we hadn't yet told them we still had to pretend to be a happy couple. We nodded and laughed together through gritted teeth as they chuckled and chatted and invited us to parties and dinners that we both knew we would never be going to. After a few more nights of prickly tensions I packed up my bare essentials and moved in with my friend Janice. Her house was far from ideal, for a start she didn't even have a couch, she only had single chairs, so I either had to curl up to the point of cramp or use her hard wooden floorboards.

A couple of days after I had left I got a text to say that she was moving out. She had never really liked London and now that we had split there wasn't a lot to keep her there. I felt guilty, so I gave her all of the time and space that she needed so that she could get her things together while I continued living on Janice's floor. It was a total mess of a fortnight, but by the end of it she had moved out, our 'break' had officially become a break up, our four years of shared history had come to an end, and my quarter life crisis was underway...

***

The point I can't stress enough is that I never wanted to become the person you're reading about. As much as I would like to I can't even try to blame anyone else. It was a dramatic change, but it wasn't as if it happened overnight, so it's not as if I couldn't have done anything to stop it. What follows is a story that begins in a comfortable, leafy, North London flat and sees me waking up with strangers, passing out in a field, losing my job and being forced out of my home.

A lot of my problems began shortly after my last birthday, put simply I didn't enjoy turning 25. I usually like birthdays, but I had approached that one with the same level of caution that I would reserve for defusing a landmine in a sandpit. I didn't even want anyone to get excited on my behalf so I went out of my way not to mention it, and I actually had a very low key and pretty miserable day. Penelope was disappointed, she had wanted to go all out for me and take me away for the weekend and do something special, but I didn't want to. Instead I went to work and afterwards we went for a mediocre meal followed by the cinema. I can't even remember what film we saw, but I remember it being crap.

The main reason for my trepidation was because 25 seemed like such a scary age; by 25 you should probably have graduated and you should be firmly on route to your career. By 25 you will probably have had your first love, and you will almost certainly have had your first break-up. By the time you're 25 you've come to know the person you think you are and by 25 you'll have come to know the multiple people who you're not.

Since graduating with a first class accountancy degree I had worked as a low to mid- level drone for a multinational banking empire. It may pay reasonably well but finance isn't for everyone; in fact it's only really for extremely tough people or, even worse, the kind of people who prefer to have money than friends. In short, finance is for the kind of people who can forfeit the temptation of waking up smiling for the prospect of sleeping easy.

The company that I worked for was based in one of the big imposing glass towers that dominate the skyline. The company itself may have been sprawling and complex, but my job was mechanical, de-personalised and extremely easy to do. Everything that I did relied on a complete sense of emotional detachment in order to give me any sense of satisfaction. Despite my reservations I had found myself playing the role of a pawn in a capitalist chess game that I didn't really want to be a part of.

It was never meant to end up like that.

***

When I was a teenager I spent many long enlightening evenings listening to Morrissey and reading an enormous amount of books. It was around the time that I first read Catcher in the Rye that I utterly fell in love with literature. From that day onwards I spent almost every cold winter evening wrapped up with a mug of coffee and a book. I also spent far too many long summer days in Hampstead Heath with only the sunshine and the words of Joyce, Dickens, Nabakov and Elliott as my company.

It wasn't just fiction that I immersed myself in. While I was a student I sent myself on a three year intellectual crash course in self discovery that included a sampling of every ist and every ism that I could find. I joined all of the different political societies, where I argued into the early hours of the morning and took part campus protests against student fees and foreign wars, but regardless of my ideological explorations I always came away with 10 times as many questions as answers.

By the time that I graduated my literary senses and political curiosities were higher than ever, but graduating into a recession meant that I would inevitably become far too compromised to maintain the same level of self-righteousness and far too cynical to be so ideological. I've always been somewhat of a realist. One of the main reasons that I had studied accountancy was for the security that I thought it could offer me, but after only a few days in the big bad world of work I already wished that I could go back in time and do a history degree. What I like about the humanities is that they are about choices and individuality, and they can either help you to build an empire or leave you flipping burgers in McDonalds. In contrast even the best accountancy degree can only take you in one direction.

At its heart this story is as much about my dissatisfaction with my circumstances as it is about anything else. It wasn't just my job that I was sick of, it was everything else too. Everything just felt so banal and removed from where I wanted to be. At the stage where this story begins my former dreams couldn't have felt any further away. That's why in my more extreme moments I felt like I had to change almost everything about me.

As well as that this is also a story about women, and there are four in particular who have dominated my life over these last few months. There was Penelope and my friend Janice, but there were also Sophie and Venus, and if this story has heroines then it's definitely them. Before my crisis I don't think that I had ever even been in the position to be unfaithful, let alone in the position to break multiple hearts within a matter of months.

Until I met Penelope I had always been terrible around girls, I found them really hard to talk to. I get nervous around new people, it's not because I'm ugly; my face wasn't exactly hand painted by God, but it doesn't look like it was drawn by

Picasso either. It's nothing to do with how I look; it's because of how I act. One of main the reasons is because I have a certain annoying quality about me and my voice goes high whenever I get nervous. It's not just that though, it's also that I also tend to gesticulate when I talk, to the point that when I'm excited my hands flap around like a pair of flailing fish.

To make matters worse I also get nosebleeds. I get them a lot. I get them whenever I'm anxious, worried, nervous or scared. I've had them on busy trains, I've had them during exams and I even got one during my three month review at work. As I was breaking up with her I could feel the familiar pre bleed itch coming on and then my mind crystallised and I focused on a thought that had been going through my head for days, what were the odds that someone like me, a limp wristed accountant who gets spontaneous nosebleeds, could ever meet a girl better than her?

***

"Why are you doing this?" she asked. There wasn't really a good way to answer; I had already failed in my attempt to let her down gently, so instead I decided that I had to be as honest and direct as possible. "I'm not in love with you anymore", I said. BOOM! She was winded. I had tried to respond as calmly and soberly as I could, but I knew that I had just thrown her a big metaphorical punch.

***

At the time I knew that I was taking an incredible risk. I knew that I was potentially throwing away four years of relative happiness on what could turn out to be a whim. I was afraid of change but I knew that I had to break out of my comfort zone and get back in touch with who I wanted to be. When I looked at her I still loved her but not in the same way that I once had, and not in the same way that I wanted to.

I went round to see her off. It was an incredibly reticent and English farewell, so we didn't even share a hug or exchange much more than a sorry glance. Despite our repression I had a horrendous lump in my throat as she drove away from the flat for the last time. Within a matter of weeks she had moved down to Brighton, where she quickly got herself a good job that paid her a lot of money, and soon she had fallen back in love with life.

I didn't handle things quite so well...

Chapter 2

That Sunday I met Steven and Janice for wine. Sunday Night Wine had become a regular part of our week, it was a chance for us to reflect and vent about the week that was, and to mentally prepare ourselves for the one that would follow. It was a gloriously depressing ritual; nobody ever brought good news, and if they did then we barely even gave it lip service. The problem was that it felt like we had so many things to moan about. We're from the generation who have been sold out by Labour, trampled on by Conservatives and given away to the corporate economy for a rock-bottom price. Our hopes had been thwarted by economic downturn and our days felt unfulfilled, although none of that doom and gloom kept us from enjoying the simple pleasures of cigarettes, wine and one-another's company.

At that point Janice was a deeply unhappy woman; she felt undervalued, undersexed and underpaid. She was incredibly clever and multi-talented, she was wasting herself in the City, and she knew it. Her dissatisfaction had become one of her defining characteristics, it underpinned everything from the permanent pout she wore to the utmost level of care she took not to put on any make-up whatsoever before going to work.

Her dissatisfaction had been with her all her life, but her crisis had only properly been triggered when she moved to London. She didn't grow up around here, she grew up in a small affluent town in the Home Counties and she came from that sort of family who voted for Thatcher, sent their daughters to single-sex private schools and worried about God, so it's fair to say that she had a sheltered childhood. She was very ambitious though, and she left school with all A's and went to study in Edinburgh. She worked hard as a student and graduated with another set of straight A's, a pair of big Bambi eyes, a head full of high expectations and a lust for life. She moved down to London for the money and glamour that everyone expects to find, but instead she found isolation, boredom and an ever growing dependence on anti depressants.

She used to have hopes, ambitions and dreams of being a writer. But after a couple of years in the city she had traded-in her love life, social life and artistic dreams for reasonable money and tied back hair. She had lost so much of her sparkle, and she felt so lost. The city is full of beautiful people and glamorous tourists, everyone seems to know everyone else and she felt like there wasn't any room for a quiet loner like her. Whenever she looked around she saw lots of superficially happy couples and good looking people with everything going for them. Having come from a small town she had never felt as insignificant and unloved as she did when she was being shoved around by anonymous city centre crowds like a big lonely piece of meat.

When she originally moved down she lived in a small single bedroom flat that overlooked Clapham Common. The setting and the scene were perfect, but unfortunately it was too expensive, and after three months of hammering her overdraft she decided that she couldn't afford it anymore. Her next step was to move into a tightly packed flat with five other girls in a bohemian part of Islington. There were plenty of art galleries and wine bars but her flat was tiny, and all of the noise, the mess and the parties made her feel like she had regressed back to student halls. She knew straight away that it was an awful idea, so she left girl hell after only a month. Finally, after she had been given her first pay rise, she moved into a humble studio flat in West Hampstead.

Steven's a different story. He lives in a big modern flat in a nice part of Camden with two other financial sector types. I have absolutely no idea how they can afford to live there because the rent is excessive, and although his salary was a little bit higher than mine it still wasn't anywhere near high enough to make it sustainable. The difference in our salaries was reflective of the depressing fact that technically speaking he was senior to me, although thankfully I never actually had to work directly for him, which would be too much to bear. One of the big differences between us was that he was actually pretty good at what he did, although his interest had been waning for a while. The problem was that he didn't care for the company any longer, the only reason he ever did in the first place was because he wanted to move to London and they offered him a good relocation package. At first he tried to be a company man and there was a short period after he first joined that he had visions of staying for a few years and working his way up to become a partner, but that enthusiasm was slowly and surely sucked out of him by far too many long boring afternoons of nothing happening. The daily grind took its toll, although at that point neither of us could have predicted how sour his departure would be.

His main problem is that he's built up a picture of who he wants to be in his head, and he won't allow himself to do anything that deviates or detracts from that image. The difficulty he has is that the image that he's aspiring to relies on him having the business acumen of Donald Trump and the sex appeal of James Bond. He tries his best though, and he has a big car, a designer wardrobe and a massive widescreen TV. Everything in his house is new and his kitchen is full of culinary delights and posh stuff from Selfridges and Borough Market, but it still doesn't quite cut the mustard. Janice has known him far longer than I have and says that he's always been that way. He was brought up in a strict and recently gentrified military family who had reputations to build and money to burn, so it's not a great shock that he expressed himself through cockiness, arrogance and consumerism. The problem is that although he might be an excellent economist with other people's money, he's hopeless with his own. He had already built up tens of thousands of pounds of debt from trying to live a millionaire's lifestyle on what was only marginally better than a graduate salary.

He's not happy either, he feels like he's been robbed of a glamorous life in an alternative universe where he can rule the world based on his good looks, and where self destruction is a virtue. He doesn't want to talk about his feelings, so he tries to drink them away, it's not rare for him to be drunk four nights a week and at least tipsy on one of the others. There are lots of other manifestations of his inner-demons, he may not use happy-pills but he has definitely tried to hurt himself. He thinks that I've never noticed the cuts on the insides of his arms. If they're not tell-tale signs of dysfunction or unhappiness then I don't know what is. They're the sort of lifestyle deformities that you have to choreograph your whole wardrobe around, they're the reason that he wears long sleeves all the time, and on the rare occasions when he doesn't he wears watches or accessories to cover them up. I've never mentioned them to him because I don't know how he would take it, and I don't know if we have that kind of friendship. Regardless of if he knows that I've seen them, what they represent is a manifestation of the humanity and doubts that even the brashest among us hold. They confirm that underneath the plastic there is a sensitive and damaged man.

Sadly he doesn't have very many places that he can turn to. He doesn't really open up enough to his friends and his love life has been one big messy catalogue of one-night stands and silly mistakes. For the last few months he had been having a chat room romance with a troubled teenager named Brogan. From what I knew she was a 17 year old gothic school girl who listened to Marilyn Manson and didn't like her parents. He always said that it was purely plutonic but I was having trouble believing him.

The point is that we all have problems, but we're friends, and you have to be there for your friends. When you're unhappy there can be an affinity that comes from being around other people who are unhappy. To subvert that time honoured cliché, I found that their misery gave me company. We're united by our disillusionment and our disappointment; we're all middle class, we're all white and a few years ago we could have grown up to run the world. The problem is that all of the lofty opportunities that we would have had a few years ago have gone, and they've been replaced by institutionalised mediocrity and low expectations. The crash changed everything, if our parents were the first generation to grow up without God then we're the first to grow up without any hope, and that's far more dangerous.

***

That Sunday we met in a nice wine bar on a brightly lit backstreet near to Regents Park. It was a cold night outside and unfortunately the conversation at our table wasn't a great deal warmer. "So basically guys," began Janice, "everything is fucked," she may have been speaking hyperbolically but she did have a reason to be wound up that day. "What the fuck are those fucking fuckers playing at promoting that horse faced bitch over me? I wonder who she had to sleep with to fix that appointment." Even though her language was foul her point was valid, she was much better at her job than Sophie. She was also right about her other point, Sophie had actually been hooking up with the head of the appointment committee for weeks.

Janice hated Sophie. In her eyes she represented everything that was wrong with women in the City. On the face of it she was just another accountant version of Barbie whose shallow, never ending quest for promotion was based on nothing more than a combination of vanity and her ability to look the other way while men took advantage of her. Janice believed that people like her were complicit in ensuring that good women would always be overlooked in favour of silly little girls who could barely string a sentence together but understood how to say the word yes. It was an ingrained part of our company culture that for women to get promoted they had to conform to every single male expectation. The reason why Janice could only get so far was because she spoke her mind and she wouldn't let anyone slap her on the ass. In contrast Sophie was younger than her, more glamorous than her and didn't have enough of a backbone to keep her below the glass ceiling.

Steven was pretty calm about the whole thing. "Sexual politics is sexual politics", he said, "and we have to be realistic. If she stops then he'll have her sacked and she knows it. It's no different to the hundreds of other scenarios that are unfolding across our industry every single day. For him it's a case of kicking back and taking advantage of the situation while she has to grin and bear it." We both knew that he was right; it was effectively a combination of salacious gossip and entrenched misogyny that ran our offices. "I mean don't get me wrong," he continued, "she's quite good looking and I certainly wouldn't say no, but when it comes to work she's extremely under qualified and she knows absolutely nothing about the state of the economy or the fragile times we're living in. When you look into her eyes you don't see someone that commands your respect and fills you with confidence, you see someone who looks terrified."

While I poured more wine he shifted the conversation away from the topic of whether or not he would like to have sex with Sophie and onto the more pertinent matter of Penelope. "So it's been a couple of week, you can spill the beans. Who are you seeing now?" I sighed; even though I had already told him otherwise he still found it inconceivable that I could have broken up with her without having someone else lined up. I shook my head and tried to ignore him, but he was like a demented gossip-seeking blood hound that had just found the scent of some scandal.

"There's really nobody else, I promise. I know that it may seem pretty far out and whacky and I'm sorry to disappoint you, but I'm telling the truth, I'm just single."

"Then that makes it even worse", he was genuinely stunned. "I mean what the hell is the point of working a 10 or 12 hour day without the promise of some fun along the way?" He leaned back and paused for breath before he continued to impart his chauvinistic wisdom on to me. "Let's just be honest about everything and start to call a spade a spade. You and Penelope met at University, but that was years ago, you've grown up and you're in the real world now. This is when you have to stop all of your miserable old man bullshit and get out there."

I exchanged a 'here we go again' glance with Janice and shrugged my shoulders.

Suddenly something clicked and a light bulb went off in his head. "Wait a minute", he said as if he had solved an age old mystery or accidentally stumbled across the meaning of life. "I know exactly what this is all about. I know why you're being so whiny and pathetic about it all. I would be happy to bet you anything in the world that it's because you've never even been with anyone other than Penelope have you?"

"Fuck off Steven," I snapped defensively, even though it's not as if my sexual history was anything to be ashamed of.

"I honestly can't believe this", he said, "you total sad bastard, you need to get laid now." I shook my head and rolled my eyes dismissively. "Anyway" he said, "forgetting all of that bullshit, the point that I was originally trying to make was that what we do is not easy. It can be really hard work and we deserve to enjoy ourselves. It's only going to get harder from here too because the company are doing almost everything wrong. What you have to remember is that our business was run by straight white men for years, but now all of that contemptuously PC New Labour bullshit has happened and there are air-headed women like Sophie in the boardroom and foreigners are being used to fill quotas. With that as our backdrop it's no wonder the economy is in ruins."

There was a short pause before Janice intervened. "So bearing all of that in mind, how are you feeling about your review?" His annual review was only a few days away and there had been rumours of mass redundancies going around for a while. He was a bit thrown by the question so he let his smile turn into something a bit more contemplative.

"I won't get a pay rise that's for sure. But I should be ok. Despite economic necessity they haven't really got rid of all that many of us, and if we're being fair then there are at least 1000 people that they should cut before they even think about axing me."

"I know that, but they've stopped being a rubber stamping exercise" she said. "My last one was really scary. They've set me a host of ridiculous new targets that I can't possibly reach so that it gives them a good excuse and an easy way to get rid of me if they need to. Do you remember what happened to Tony? He came in early every single day, he beat all of his targets and he worked himself to the bone, and yet they still got rid of him didn't they?" Tony had been one of our colleagues who had started in a graduate position at the same time as I had. He had worked around the clock and had done everything that was asked of him, but that hadn't stopped him from being fired after an argument with one of the team leaders. After that he was blacklisted across the sector and now he works in an electronics shop on Tottenham Court Road and he isn't even getting interviews for any of the jobs he's applying for.

Steven didn't want to talk about it anymore so he let his apprehensive eyes stray from ours and locked them on to those of a voluptuous blonde woman in a short skirt who was standing at the bar. It wasn't a mistake, he had actually been trying to make eye contact with her since we had sat down, but she had only just noticed. She smiled at him and waved him over like a dog. "Excuse me", he said as he stood up, "I'll be back in a minute."

Janice shook her head a little and applied a fresh layer of lipstick. "I'm really sorry about that Floyd. I know that it'll go fine and that he won't get fired, but I wanted to take him down a peg or two."

"That's ok" I said, "He's being a bit more of an arse than usual though. I'm assuming that there must be more to it than just his review."

"There is" she said, "and to be fair most of his other problems are a bit more serious."

He never told me very much about what was really going on in his life, instead he only told me about the good parts. However he did talk to her, and from speaking to her I knew that his debts were getting out of control, and I knew that his way of coping was to pretend it wasn't happening and descend even further into the kind of consumer heaven where his TV was massive, his morals were loose and his pleasures were instant. We both knew that his situation was only going to get worse, and in the back of our minds we knew that we would probably have to be there to pick up the pieces.

We glanced across the bar and saw that he was already flirting very heavily with the lucky girl. It was a sight that we had both seen multiple times before; he was using one of his famous 'routines.' To an untrained eye it would look like a natural conversation, but in fact it wasn't. Everything that he was doing was choreographed around the goal of getting her into his bed by the quickest and least personal means available. We had both seen this particular routine lots of times before; he would have introduced himself to her and began by chatting about nothing in particular, although he would have found a way to mention that he worked for a FTSE 100 company. After a few minutes he would have leaned in closer to 'hear her' and then he would accidentally stumble and would coincidentally find himself with his arm around her. That unsubtle manoeuvre would serve as his excuse to get closer to her, and then finally he would have bought her a drink to 'apologise'.

"He's so obvious. There isn't even an attempt to be anything other than shamefully transparent. Please tell me that not all women are in to that kind of thing."

"Not all of us are. Some of us like intelligence, sensitivity and romance in our men, but they're not the kind of girls that he goes for."

"How do you define the sort of girl that he goes for?"

"They're usually the kind of girls who'll grow up to wreck other people's marriages."

"So where do you fit in on the spectrum?" I asked.

"I would love to be able to tell you that I only ever go for kind, caring and decent men, but I don't. My standards are dangerously low and I've gone for all sorts of oddballs. I've been with so many unbelievably crap men and I have no idea why I keep doing it to myself." This was definitely an understatement. Her past boyfriends had ranged from the hapless and daft right through to the downright disastrous. Things had been pretty quiet for her recently though, so she was far more used to being alone than I was, but she still hated it.

"What am I going to do?" I asked, "I'm not used to being single, what happens if I end up going off the wall and it makes me act like him?"

She snorted in to her wine at the very thought of it. "You will never end up like him" she said. "If you do then I'll have to find new friends, because I promise that this would be the last time that we ever went out anywhere together."

I smirked as she put her lipstick away and let out a big dramatic sigh, "I still want out of it all" she said. "I'm so bored of it. The bubble has burst, Thatcherism is long gone and Wall Street is dead. We all have mountains of debt and precious little to show for it, we're in stagnation and it seems like the only people with any kind of future in our industry are girls like Sophie and men like Steven." She sighed again, "When I wake up in the morning I just can't be bothered getting out of bed anymore. I look at the clock and I calculate the latest possible minute that I can leave the house. I don't remember the last time I really enjoyed what I do. Nobody cares anymore, it's like our feelings are immaterial as long as we're making money. You know, it just feels like we're all trapped at the bottom of this gigantic great big mound of shit, and every time it feels like we might be about to escape the mound it just gets bigger and bigger."

Despite every desire on my part to avoid it she also wanted to talk about Penelope, it gave her comfort to know that I was having a hard time too. "So how are you feeling?" she asked.

I thought about how I should answer, I knew that she wanted to see some red emotional meat but I wasn't at the stage of being able to serve it up. "I don't think it's really set in yet", I said. "I was with her for a long time and obviously we lived together and everything so it's been hard. I can barely even remember what living alone is like. But now that I'm back to being on my own everything has changed." There wasn't a lot more that I wanted to add. "It's not that I stopped caring about her, in a way I still love her and probably always will. It's just that I felt like if we didn't break up then there was a small chance that we would have stayed together forever."

"Would that have been so bad?" she asked.

"It wouldn't have been bad as such. It would have been fine. But that's the problem. I don't want things to be fine, I'm too idealistic. I've seen what my parents are like around each other and I want to be better than that."

"Well I think that you did the right thing," she said sympathetically. "You did what you thought was right, even thought it was hard. Besides, it could have gone a lot worse. Speaking of a lot worse, I'm going on an internet date next Saturday and I can already tell that it's going to be totally awful. He's nothing special when we talk online and I have no reason to think that he's going to be any better in person."

"So why are you meeting him?" I asked.

"It's because he's my free tester." That was probably the most tragic sentence I had ever heard. She laughed at the ridiculousness of what she had just said, "and also because I genuinely don't have anything better to do with my night. Please tell me that you're doing something more inspiring."

"Not really", I said, "and if I can't find anything better then I might just tag along in secret and watch your monstrosity of a night unfolding."

"I don't know what would be more depressing, the idea of spending your Saturday night on a blind date with your free tester from a website that was designed to help single people interact, or the idea of spending your Saturday night watching somebody else out on a date with their free tester from a website that was designed to help single people to interact."

"I think I'll go with the latter" I ventured, "although I'm sure that I'll manage to put together something equally thrilling."

"I'm sure you will" she said, "It's just that my night already feels totally and utterly pointless and it's still six days away." She took another sip of wine, "It's also that my inner snob keeps on reminding me that I never thought that I would become the sort of person who uses dating websites."

"Who are you defining as the sort of people who use dating websites?" I asked.

"Lonely people" she said, "and I've realised that I'm one of them. It's taken a lot for me to admit it because I've always tried to tell myself that I'm so independent. Until recently I always thought that the archetypal question of our generation was to ask where we're going, but when I look around me now I realise that it should be to ask where we are."

I nodded and we finished our drinks in silence.

Chapter 3

Needless to say Janice's blind date went terribly. To be fair, her expectations had been so incredibly low to begin with that it meant it would be hard for her to have been too disappointed. It began badly when he was over 20 minutes late in meeting her and didn't even bother to text let alone apologise. As she sat alone in $tarbucks she kept debating how much longer she would wait, but she kept giving him an extra two minutes on the off-chance that he might be her Prince Charming who could whisk her away on his metaphorical horse and save her from ever having to pay to organise an online date. In the end she wasn't so fortunate, he eventually strutted in devoid of charisma and smelling of the same kind of aftershave her dad wore, and then he smiled awkwardly and presented her with a bunch of fake plastic flowers. At first she thought that they may have been intended as some kind of joke, but then he told her that they were better than the real thing because they would last longer.

After his late and mean spirited introduction they went to a touristy chain restaurant in Leicester Square. She had a stodgy salad and some oily pasta, while he had an exceptionally dry steak. However, as bad as it was, the food was still 1000 times better than their conversation. They didn't have anything in common so it was a horribly awkward night that was made up of really mundane time filling questions that they didn't really care about the answers to (things like 'what are your favourite films?' and 'do you like living in London?') When they weren't exchanging banalities they were sitting in silence and secretly wishing that the ground beneath could open up and swallow them.

Their night ended with an uncomfortable kiss outside the train station. His kissing technique was unique to say the least, and when she was telling me about him she likened it to a cross between a faulty washing machine and a wet fish. Before he left she took the unilateral decision of killing off any chance of a second date by giving him a fake mobile number. When she got home she dumped the 'flowers', blocked his email address and removed him from her Facebook page.

***

My night wasn't much better. I spent most of it with Steven and his repulsive flatmate Kenneth. Kenneth is an absolute moron, although that's actually an insult to morons. He works for an executive headhunting company and lives up to every single bad City boy stereotype; he's shallow, he's vain, he's cutthroat, he's right wing to the point of bordering on racism and he drinks and snorts far too much. He's extremely unpleasant to be around and he has an extremely vicious streak that turns the worst excesses of misogyny and intolerance into an art form. "Floyd you miserable bastard", he said as he hugged me, "Steven says you've been screwed over by some bitch, well don't worry because we're going to get you hammered."

***

I had been talked into spending my afternoon shopping with Steven in Knightsbridge as part of a mission that we called Operation Trendy Floyd. Although he has always been very conscientious about his own appearance he spent that day being almost obsessive in his desire to ensure that I 'looked right'. He was like a man possessed, it was as if he had been overcome by a sense of fashion derived humanitarianism and he was determined to rescue me from the dreary clutches and dire social consequences of having a boring M&S dominated wardrobe. After a few long hours he had taken me around almost every single one of the same vacuous department stores that I had spent the last 25 years trying to avoid.

Going shopping with him can be an enlightening experience, his mind wanders as he considers the 'texture', 'message' and 'meaning' of every single item and studies them in near forensic detail. The upside is that he can be unintentionally funny when talks about the 'core narratives' or 'structural strengths' of a new tie. However, it also means that it takes about 10 times longer than it should as he stops to consider every single individual item in terms of the wider contexts of his wardrobe, his home and exactly how it might fit into the rest of his life.

In the end we must have visited about 15 different shops and all that I left with was an overpriced pair of purposefully faded and stylistically torn jeans that looked like an angry designer had taken a broken bottle to them. He told me that it was OK, but his dismissive tone and sulky slouch made it purposefully clear that he was disappointed in me. Never one to mope, he alleviated his frustrations by buying a pair of Jack Wills loafers, a hideous green designer belt that was made from hemp and a new I-Pad.

***

We started the night in a nice vibrant little pub just off Portobello Road. The only problem was that I couldn't stand being around Kenneth. Aside from his generally obnoxious tone he is also extremely stupid, especially for someone who is paid to know about what's going on in the world. I have never seen anyone look as unjustifiably proud as he did when he smugly announced that he had never voted. Not only was he obnoxious and stupid, he was also lazy, it sounded like he did even less work than we did. He kept talking about some of the supposedly great 'frapes' he and his colleagues did to each other. I cringed as he told me; I hate it when people talk as if changing someone's Facebook status is even remotely comparable to raping them. Thankfully it only took a few minutes before he abandoned us after predictably latching onto the drunkest looking girl in the whole pub. She was barely standing up straight as he got her in his predatory sights and went over to 'help' her. I thought about telling the security guards, but it wasn't long before they noticed what was going on – after a couple of minutes I saw them closing in on him then dragging him out kicking and screaming.

Steven was on his phone at the time and I had no interest in getting involved, so I decided not to tell him. It wouldn't have mattered anyway as it wasn't long before he decided to follow him in abandoning me for the prospect of female company. We were midway through talking about how much I hated the fact that as long as I lived in London I could never afford to own my own home. Although to be honest it was more of a monologue than a conversation, and it was obvious that he was just nodding politely and waiting for me to pause for breath so that he could find an excuse to stop having to pretend to listen.

As soon as I had finished he nodded slowly and then turned his attention towards a pretty looking blonde girl who was standing at the bar. He smiled knowingly at me and went over to begin one of his routines. "Oh my God," he proclaimed, "I'm sorry to bother you but I just wanted to tell you how beautiful you are," he paused for effect, "wait a minute, I'm sure I've seen you somewhere before." I knew exactly where he was going with this one, "are you famous? Wait a minute, you are, aren't you? Are you that model?" She started giggling like a school girl, which was his signal to keep going. Sure enough it worked, and within a few minutes she had left all of her friends and joined us.

Watching him around women is hilariously vulgar, and it makes me so glad that I don't have a sister for him to hit on. It's mainly vulgar because it's so obscenely pornographic and empty. He assumes absolutely no intelligence whatsoever on the part of the girl he's pursuing. Instead he assumes that she must be as submissive, superficial and easily impressed as the girls you see in movies. In contrast I had never even had a one night stand - I suppose I had always assumed that if a girl was willing to have sex within the first few months of knowing me then there almost certainly had to be something wrong with her. Needless to say my standards were about to slip dramatically, but at least I had them in the first place.

My role was easy, for the duration of this routine I was meant to be as quiet and passive as that guy you see on Oxford

Street with the giant sign that points to the golf shop. All things considered I was a pretty good at it; I smiled, I pretended to laugh at his jokes and I rarely uttered a syllable that wasn't being done solely to enforce the idea of how much better he was than us mere mortals.

My state of non-existence must have lasted for about 20 minutes before she got up to go to the bar. It was mere seconds after she had walked away that he leaned across the table and beckoned me over to whisper in my ear. "We have to go" he said quietly, "it turns out that she has a kid." This was our queue to leave.

***

Soon enough we were reunited with a very drunk and slightly bruised Kenneth, who had just taken a pill that he had been sold by a homeless man outside the pub. We went to the newsagents and picked up a couple of cans and then went to a small reggae nightclub which had an abundance of drugs and an almost exclusively Jamaican clientele. The security guards eyed us up and checked us for knives, this was probably the only night club in the world where middle class white people were the ones who the security considered to be a danger. Our reunion didn't last long, it was only another quarter of an hour or so before we lost him again because he had drank too much and had passed out in a delirious mess in the corner. In a sharp contrast with his friend's state of wooziness Steven was a clear sighted and focused man with a very important mission; he had decided that he was desperate to 'shack up' with a black woman, and he refused to go home until he had.

Unfortunately this fine equality-promoting gesture of multiculturalism wasn't to be his only goal for the night. He had also decided that he wanted to get me 'pilled'. "Go on mate, underneath all of our bullshit we're all pretty much the same and pills just help you to realise that. Just try it this once, go on you'll love it" he sneered with such a lack of personal control that he was almost foaming at the mouth. "You need to give it a go", he said, "and then you need to get yourself some action before your virginity grows back." At that point I knew that it was going to be a long night...

It was only a few minutes later that he managed to set a new record in terms of totally inconsiderate and moronic behaviour by spiking my drink. I should have seen it coming, I had been wondering why he kept insisting on buying everything, but by the time I had noticed that something was wrong I was well past the first hurdle and there was no chance of going back. I could feel the effects of what he had done as it slowly took over my body. At first my throat felt like cotton wool and then I started to feel my head spinning and my vision starting to fade. "Steven" I said with a slur, "I feel totally messed up. I think I'm going to have to stick to the water."

"Floyd you woman," he shrieked with delight, "It's so obvious that you've never been properly high before!" He could barely contain his glee as he put his arms around me and kissed me lightly on my forehead. "This is brilliant" he cackled, "You're totally pilled. Just embrace it. Over the next few hours you're going to have a weird, wonderful and potentially life-affirming odyssey, so enjoy it while it lasts. The good ship Floyd has set sail for the port of wasted, and I'll be waiting for you on the other side." His smile appeared almost hysterical as he embraced me. He hugged me closely and then he eyeballed me as he pulled away "just don't be so uptight, you've just made it to the house of love, kick back and make yourself at home. You should find a good girl, enjoy yourself and write off tomorrow as a day of recovery and well deserved rest." He kissed me on the head again and winked before leaving me stuck in my own drum and bass infused version of hell.

After a few long lost seconds I began to panic. I looked across the club in desperate search of a lifeline, but it was no use. Kenneth was still in a lifeless heap on the floor, and when I finally saw Steven again he was waving at me from the other side of the room while he danced with a group of strangers

The backing track was some bouncy rap song about liking fast cars and being famous: *"GIVE ME A CAR AND KEEP IT REAL, I'LL GO CRAZY BEHIND THE GOD-DAMMED WHEEL!"* It was quite possibly among the worst songs that I had ever heard, but that didn't stop everyone who had been standing aside suddenly rushing onto the dance floor. I wanted to be sick. I needed to escape. I shoved my way through the sea of tightly-packed sweaty bodies as I wandered startled, bewildered and in need of an exit. The building design was architecturally illiterate; there were signs that pointed towards nothing and stairs that went nowhere. I practically crawled to the edge of the floor. Then I dragged myself up and managed a few heavy steps, but I was still totally out of my head and I had no idea how to stop it. I momentarily lost all strength as I slouched down on to my knees and slid down a drink soaked wall. *"YOU'VE GOT THE BEER, I'VE GOT THE WEED, LET'S GET SOME WHEELS AND WE'LL HAVE EVERYTHING WE NEED!"* I knew that it couldn't possibly end well. My legs were shaking and my knees were preparing to give way. Meanwhile a trusty old nosebleed had built up right on queue. I was grateful for the small mercy that came from the glimmer of familiarity that I felt as the warm blood ran down my chin. I smiled as the taste reminded me that I was still alive. Then the music faded to white noise and the lights dimmed to grey, and then finally everything went black.

Chapter 4

When I woke up I felt horrendous. My mind was a nauseous jumble of mess and I was stiff with worry as I took in my unfamiliar new surroundings. I was dehydrated and disconcerted, and I was in a room that I had never seen before. The covers were a thick pastel shade of red and the walls surrounding me were lined with bright pink and eggshell stripes. There was a half open window and a slither of daylight that peered through the thin brown curtains and allowed a small crack of radiance into the room. I gave myself a few seconds to take it in before I rolled over to the edge of the bed. I eased myself up, but as soon as I was standing I felt like I was ready to collapse. My head was pounding, but I persevered, and after what felt like an age I made my way over to the window. When I pulled back the curtains and looked outside I saw a quaint and leafy suburban street and I heard the sounds of birds chirping in the distance.

As I looked around me I saw an en-suite bathroom, a desk with a pile of biology text books, a bean bag with a giant fuzzy teddy bear on it and a row of empty beer bottles. There were a combination of posters of pop stars, Escher drawings and periodic tables all over the walls, which lead me to put two and two together and conclude that I must have spent the night with a student. For a couple of seconds I felt pretty cool, and then it sank in that I had absolutely no recollection of anything that had happened.

I was only wearing my pants but I could see the rest of my clothes in an untidy heap on the floor. When I got my blackberry out of my jeans I saw that it was just after 9am and I had three missed calls from Steven. I also had a text that read *'hey! I am so proud of you!!! I have no idea what got into you!!! All of a sudden you were like some kind of social suicide bomber!!! And it worked!!! I saw you leaving the club with an utterly stunning girl!!! Nice one ;-)'*

I had absolutely no idea who he was talking about.

I knew that the honourable thing to do would surely be to wait for a while and find out. I didn't quite feel ready to see anyone, but I wanted to know a little bit more. I opened the bedroom door a-jar and peered into the hallway. I couldn't hear any voices but it definitely appeared to be an all girls flat; the walls were all the same pink and eggshell design and there was a bunch of newly picked flowers on a table by the front door.

There was no way to know if she was actually there, but I didn't feel like I was ready to find out. I bit down on my lip and went back into the bedroom, then I hunted for my phone and tried to call Steven, but it went straight through to his voicemail.

I put my clothes back on and thought about what I could do. I found myself pacing the room for a while before going over to her desk and using her stationery to write a small note that simply said *'sorry about last night'* and then I fled the scene. Thankfully her room was on the ground floor so it meant that I could climb out of the window, if she had been higher up then I don't know what I would have done. After I had escaped I ran until I found the nearest tube station.

***

It turned out that I was at the wrong side of town, with that in mind I went to a nearby McDonalds so that I could clean up a bit before I got on the train. As I walked in I was hit by the overpowering smell of fried breakfasts and plastic furniture and it made me feel like I was about to throw up. I didn't like it at all, but I held my nose and navigated my way through the assault course of morning munchers so that I could find the toilet. When I eventually found it I discovered that there wasn't a mirror, although thankfully there was a sink, so at least I was able to splash some water on my face. I washed my hands and ran them through my thick greasy hair, and then I locked myself in the cubicle so that I could take a minute to check the underground map on my phone and find out the quickest route back home.

The cubicle itself was foul; there was a toxic smell all around me and it was covered in bigoted graffiti and fresh morning urine, all things considered they couldn't have made it any less hygienic if they had tried. I used up almost all of the toilet paper as I had to cover the seat before I could sit down. Once I had found out the quickest way back (which involved getting three different trains) I put my head in my hands and tried to clear my mind.

My moment of introspection didn't last long, after about 15 seconds of peace and reflection I was interrupted by someone who was trying to open the door. When he noticed that it was locked he tried again, I don't know why he thought that the second time would be any different. I heard a loud groaning sound as the same man started banging on it, "just a minute" I shouted to an exaggerated theatrical sigh. It was futile; there was no way that I was going to get any privacy, not as long as there was a weak-bladdered barbarian on the other side of the door. A few seconds later I heard someone else joining him. It wasn't long before they were both moaning impatiently. I knew that sitting in the cubicle wasn't doing me any good, so I forced myself up. I made sure that I only used one finger to lift the lid, that way I could flush away the paper that I had used to cushion my throne. Their knocking and grumbling continued, so I decided to flush away the rest of the roll as well just to annoy them. When I finally opened the door I saw a line of angry looking men, I nodded at them knowingly and tried to suppress my immature smile.

***

After leaving the 'restaurant' I bought a packet of cigarettes from a nearby supermarket and smoked two of them while I walked back to the Underground. There was a bit of commotion outside the station, a local 'character' was standing around with a bucket of fried chicken and throwing chunks at random. A big judgmental circle had formed around him as some people shook their heads in disbelief and others laughed at a man who was clearly disturbed and in need of help. A group of children had taken out their phones so that they could record the whole spectacle. I didn't want to stop and stare at him so instead I brushed through the crowds, only to be hit on the shoulder by a big chunk of chicken. I turned around, I was trying not to get too angry, I looked beyond the baying mobs and into his dark brown eyes, at first they looked scared, but then they switched to anger, "Fuck you!" he shouted. I continued to look at him and wondered what horrible chain of events could possibly have been inflicted on this man that could lead him to end up standing outside a train station in South London throwing bits of fried chicken at people.

***

I swiped my Oyster Card and headed downstairs. While I was sitting on the tube I kept thinking about him, how had his life began? Why was no-one looking after him? Then I drank a tooth shattering energy drink that I had picked up from a vending machine on the platform and read one of the free newspapers. The main story was something to do with a celebrity couple having marriage problems, which had no doubt been made worse by seeing them dissected on the front page of a tabloid newspaper. After reading about their pain I peered into my reflection on the screen of my phone and thought about how bad I would feel if I was splashed all over the newspapers. I couldn't see much, but it was obvious that I looked dreadful. I was so glad that there was no one around to take my picture.

***

When I eventually got home I had a shower and tried to call Steven again. It took me another five or six attempts before he eventually picked up. "Hello" he murmured in a suspicious kind of manner that suggested I had no right to be phoning.

"Good morning" I said sternly and deliberately, I was trying to sound authoritative but obviously something clicked and he started laughing. "Fuck you" I said, "I feel totally awful today, I just woke up in a stranger's bed at the other side of the city with a head that felt like mince," by this point he was close to hysterics. "Actually before we even talk about the girl, let's take a step back for a moment. What right did you have to spike me?"

"Chill out mate" he said, "you were being uptight. Frankly you should be thanking me for livening you up! It was safe, if it wasn't then I wouldn't have taken one too would I? I was looking out for you every step of the way, and anyway what's the problem? You had a good night and you managed to make it home in one piece didn't you?"

"Steven" I said firmly, "you drugged me."

"You're making it sound like I got you shot or something when in fact all that I did was help you to get a girl. Is that really such a crime?"

"What the hell did you give me?"

"Relax, it was just an E."

"You gave me an E? You gave me an E? What in the hell were you thinking?"

"There's absolutely nothing wrong with E? I got them from a good source so there were no funny chemicals or anything like that. Besides, nobody dies from them anymore, it's not the 1990s."

"They're extremely dangerous" I shouted.

"Will you listen to yourself? You're being all pompous and loud about it when all I wanted to do was get you laid."

"I know, and I'm worried that you may have succeeded at it."

"Undoubtedly," he said, "last night was a crowning achievement for you. Oh my god you should have seen how into her you were, it was quite sweet really."

"Who the hell was she?"

"I don't know, she was just a girl."

"What was she like?"

"I'm not going to lie" he began, "you were totally punching above your weight. She was gorgeous, and on any other day she would have been totally out of your league. You needed the power of the E to awaken something that stirred you into action. You did really well, I was proud of you, when I saw you leaving I felt like a proud father watching his son going to his first prom."

"Thanks mate, I suppose that in the great scheme of things it doesn't come close to making it any better, but it's a bonus of sorts."

"Don't mention it" he said conceitedly, obviously the implicit sarcasm of my comment was lost on him. "It was a great thing for you. In fact it was almost spiritual. It's all happened now so you're free to do whatever you want. Now that you've lost your inhibitions you're truly liberated, you've finally broken out of your dark, gloomy, negative headspace and into the zone. You should consider this moment to be your awakening and think of me as your prophet. Anyway I am knackered and I've got lots that I need to do so I'm going to have to go. I know that you're not happy with me but well done anyway", he yawned, "have a good day and I'll see you on the other side," the line went dead.

There was a part of me that wanted to pat myself on the back. There was also a large part of me that was shocked, if we assume that something happened then she was only the second girl I had ever been with, and I didn't even know her name. This newfound sense of confusion was balanced by a feeling of deep anxiety... what if I was starting to turn into Steven?

Chapter 5

After I had hung up I went for another shower, I also took the time to moisturise and shave so that I could begin to make myself look human again. My head felt like a cannonball weighing down on my scrawny, exhausted neck. I felt like I was carrying out some form of reconstructive surgery while I tried to ease my way back into normality. It made a small improvement, but even after shower number two I still looked appalling. I studied myself in the mirror, I was all the colours of the world's bleakest rainbow; my eyes were dopey and as dark as charcoal and my finger tips were a nicotine shade of yellow, on top of that my mind was numb and empty and I felt like I might drop dead at any moment.

If I was dying then it would have to wait until after I had visited my parents. I didn't see them anywhere near enough, so not even death would have been a good enough excuse to cancel. It's not as if I went out of my way to avoid them, it's just that things were always so busy and there was never any shortage of things that needed to be done. At that point I hadn't seen them for over two months, and even then it had been a fleeting visit to help my dad with the gardening. Since then I had missed my cousin's birthday, my aunt and uncle's anniversary party and a whole host of other family events.

One of the reasons I didn't visit them very often is because they had moved away from London. Their rural odyssey began when I moved out and went to University and they moved out of our flat in Kilburn and into a small house in one of the quiet zone five suburbs. Around the time that I graduated they moved further out to the very periphery, and then one year later as I moved to Highgate they upped sticks and moved to the countryside. Living in London is one big expensive cycle; when we're young we live in the outskirts and put aside as much money as we can so that when we're successful we can move into town. When we're successful we start saving as much as we can so that we can afford to escape town and move back out to the suburbs.

***

At first I was relieved; against all the odds it turned out that I wasn't the worst looking person on the train that morning. I had an aura of justified smugness about me as I sat down opposite a pair of tired looking teenage girls who were obviously doing their proverbial walks of shame. They looked so beaten-down and depressed that I almost felt sorry for them. They looked like the sorts of girls you see fronting anti-binge drinking campaigns; they had puffy dresses and smeared lipstick, and they looked like they hadn't eaten anything nutritious in days. Unfortunately my feelings of quiet superiority were short-lived. After only a few seconds of basking in my comparative greatness I could overhear them making fun of me. "That guy looks really gay" one of them said while she pointed at me.

"No he doesn't," said the other, "he's far too ugly for that."

I didn't like the idea of being a witness to my own character assassination so I turned up the volume on my I-pod and sank into a deep state of music assisted ignorance. I let David Bowie serenade me with 1980s dance music whilst I tried to focus on the passing countryside, even though it all looked the same. As I looked out across the long boring landscapes I thought about how much I would hate to live out there.

***

Janice comes from a rich, uptight southern family that have silver spoons in their mouths and two cars in their garage. They're very prim and proper, but she doesn't really see a lot of her globe-trotting executive dad, and ever since her mother 'accidentally' read one of her teenage diaries she's been convinced that her daughter is permanently living on the brink of suicide. What she doesn't realise is that there are one million shades of grey between feeling upset and taking your life. It's not a nice situation, they rarely see each other and when they do they argue. Janice's sisters are both successful but choose to live at home so she's the odd one out. The fact that the rest of the family are so close only makes things worse, at least if they all hated each other then they could all be written off as dysfunctional, but the fact that she's the only fly in the ointment means that it's basically her fault.

She grew up with tough love and lots of limitations and nine o'clock curfews. Her father was actually fairly indifferent, but her mother made an art form of being controlling and every time she got home she would be asked every intrusive question in the book of totalitarian parenting (Where were you? Why were you there? What were you doing? Who were you doing it with?)

She says that none of her friends believed her when she told them what her home situation was like. There were daily confrontations and regular arguments, but they always happened behind closed doors. She had felt lonely and unable to do anything about it, and that's why she lost herself in books and learning, it was easier than playing happy families. When she showed me her photos from growing up they looked like any old childhood photos, but this is a case of when the camera does lie. Keeping up appearances is easy, and even the most warped families can learn how to pose for pictures.

Steven is another person who grew up with too many boundaries. He's the product of a stern military household, and he's also the proverbial black-sheep of his family; which is because he's the first Jones in four generations not to pick up a weapon. I don't know enough of the details to give you any great insight, but I know that Steven's dad is a cranky old major and a veteran of the Falklands. I've never met him, but when Steven gets drunk he moans about him, he says that he practically forced him into a career of fighting. He says that when he was younger he was a rebel, and he's told me that he was expelled from three different state schools, all of which were favoured by the military types. It wasn't just that he hated the idea of being in the army, he also hated school. Despite his average grades his old man still managed to pull a lot of strings and got him an offer to study PPE at Oxford, but he turned it down and went for economics at Edinburgh because he wanted to get as far away as he could.

Despite the distance things didn't get any better. He never called or visited them aside from the compulsory few days every Christmas, and as soon as he arrived in Edinburgh he changed his mobile number without telling them. The final insult came four years later he decided not to invite them to his graduation ceremony. After moving to London he changed his number again and he says that he hasn't spoken to them since.

In comparison to my friends the relationship I have with my parents seems positively natural...

***

On the face of it they're just another normal middle class couple, but looks can be deceiving. My mother seems like your typecast doting housewife and to the unsuspecting eye my father seems like any other eccentric old fashioned businessman who's become a bit too stuck in his ways. This wasn't always the case though; there was once an all too brief phase between recessions when it looked like they could be on the cusp of incredible wealth and living out their dreams. All of this was blown out of the water by 'what happened next, and since then their shares have become worthless and their reputations have been destroyed.

Despite having had a traditional socialist upbringing, complete with Bob Dylan music and Labour Party summer camps, my father is an extremely right wing man. This isn't a new thing, he used to be the chairman of his local Conservative Party and he brought me up with propaganda fuelled bed time stories that were full of unsubtle political messages that glorified the Thatcher revolution and blamed the Trade Unions for everything that was wrong with the country. A particular bed time classic that springs to mind is the story of the industrious teddy bear who began selling lemonade on street corners and soon built an empire of lemonade stands, but they all had to close because his ungrateful staff went on strike, and soon none of them had any jobs, it was a harsh economic lesson for any six year old to learn. He lived and breathed politics, he was the sort of person who couldn't be without a newspaper; he couldn't imagine the world spinning without him having an opinion on almost every single aspect of it. As far back as I can remember he had always talked about his dream of standing for parliament, and then finally one year he did.

I was 14 at the time and I've still not fully forgiven him for what happened next.

The campaign itself was a badly conceived vanity project right from the start, and within only a few days of his nomination it had become permanently derailed when a local activist went to the press with a whole host of grimy allegations. 'LOVEPIG' screamed the front page of our local paper while it recounted sordid stories about him staying late at the campaign HQ to fumble around with his interns while he promised them all glittering careers as parliamentary aides.

At the time I hated him for it. I hated the betrayal, but I also hated what it did to me. Being the son of a Tory candidate was always going to ensure that I took a bit of a beating at school, but being the son of a sleazy, seedy Tory candidate who was caught doing allsorts was much worse. I had a horrible time while I paid the social price for his indiscretions, I got nothing but endless ridicule from my 'friends', endless bullying from the usual suspects and endless nods of sympathy from all of my teachers. As a result I tried to hide, I became reclusive and spent far too long alone in my room listening to Morrissey and wishing that I could be someone else. We never really talked about it, we still haven't. I've refrained from asking him how many of the stories were true. On one hand I want to know how many lies he told, but on the other I just don't see how it would enhance my life to know whether or not he used to enjoy wearing my mother's underwear and pinning his secretary against the wall.

I can still remember the sickening feeling of the humiliation that went with having local journalists virtually camped outside the house while more and more women came out of the woodwork with equally sordid stories. It was an embarrassment for me, but the impact that it had on my mother was much worse. She was the kind of woman who used to shout at the television whenever a character in a soap opera stayed with a cheating spouse, and now she had to bravely soldier on and hold herself together while her perfect world imploded and people everywhere shouted into their newspapers at her. She forced herself to wear a brave face and all the while pretended not to be too affected by the patronising pity that everyone gave her when she said that she was standing by him. I don't know how close she came to walking out, but they've never been the same since. I remember when I was growing up I was kept awake by the disturbing sounds of them having sex through the thin walls in my childhood home, but after it all came out I found their silence far harder to sleep through. It confirmed for me that they weren't having sex, which confirmed that they weren't really talking. I guess that at their ages they were trapped in a position where it would have been too late for them to start afresh. They're both creatures of habit so they would have been too lonely by themselves, they were both retired and they had savings, so they just wanted an easy life.

There were no winners from the saga, in its own way the impact it had on him was every bit as bad as it was on her. Afterwards it was like all of his optimism had been killed and he became distant and subdued. It was a degrading and completely self-inflicted conclusion to the political dream that he had been building up to all his life.

***

My mother looked appalled as she opened the door. I smiled as she gave me that look of disappointment only mothers can. Her disappointment was quickly replaced by a mixture of sympathy and fear. She didn't say anything, but she made sure I got in as quickly as I could as she obviously didn't want the neighbours to see me. She cares too much about keeping up appearances, she isn't rich but she makes sure that every time someone comes round they eat off the best china. She went through to the kitchen while I took off my shoes by the front door. By sheer coincidence I had arrived just as the kettle was boiling, so after I hung up my jacket we all sat down with a well timed cup of tea and chatted. It was actually really nice chatting to them, none of it was particularly deep or meaningful but it was comfortable. We talked about politics, the recession and whether or not there was any chance of me getting promoted at work (there wasn't, but it was nice of them to ask.)

Unfortunately my father ruined the congenial mood by dropping the inevitable relationship shaped clanger, "I do hope Penelope will be joining us when we visit your grandmother next week." There was a pregnant pause of awkward silence before I responded. I could see his smile slowly turning into a look of cautious curiosity and then slight panic as the realisation hit him that he had said something wrong. "No she won't", I said as casually as I could, "we actually broke up a couple of weeks ago."

BOOM! Their eyebrows had risen with shock at the same time as they had fallen silent. It was a safe kind of silence though because good manners and family etiquette ensured that neither of them would ask me anything about it. Instead of saying any more I just shrugged it off and complimented the tea. Sure enough my great revelation was relegated into the background and we managed to go for most of the afternoon without it rearing its inconvenient head again. Instead we talked about TV shows, rugby and whatever was in the news that day. Like so many British families we're experts when it comes to burying our feelings, we've developed a level of collective emotional repression that can take a lifetime to achieve.

Their disappointment was understandable though. They had loved her; she was polite, well bred, and tailor made for eating mediocre cakes and laughing at family albums. I think they had always been amazed that I had managed to get someone so good. The other reason they liked her was because her existence averted one of their greatest fears...

My father in particular was always terrified that I might be gay. He's one of those old fashioned bigots who think that sexuality is defined purely by accents and music tastes. With that in mind he had noted my Morrissey albums, my lack of any previous girlfriends and the way I moved my hands while I spoke. After having put together what he saw as an unholy trinity of campness he had created the terrifying scenario that he might have a gay son. I can still remember the mixture of elation and relief in his voice when I first introduced him to Penelope. He was delighted as he took me to one side and told me in no uncertain terms that he was glad I wasn't "a fucking shirt lifter".

I'm certainly not gay, but I would be lying if I said that the thought had never crossed my mind. There were times when I was a very confused teenager; it wasn't that I liked boys, but I went through long periods of not really liking girls either. I had an inbuilt inferiority complex that made all but the plainest girls seem too unobtainable to even consider approaching, and I didn't want to approach the plainest girls because they were too plain. I remember being overcome with curiosity when I walked in on two boys I knew kissing in the toilets. I didn't want to kiss either of them, but I did want to kiss someone. Yet despite every single attempt I somehow managed to go my entire time at school without sharing a single affectionate moment with anyone.

***

It was towards the end of the day that we talked about my grandmother. She was a very old lady, she was 92, and she had lived a long and active life, but her age was catching up with her and she had been sick and poorly for a long time, which meant that she could barely remember any of it. It was clear that she was dying, and having been fortunate enough to reach 25 without losing anyone I was close to I had absolutely no idea how to confront it.

"Floyd, you have to come with us next time we visit, it might be the last time you get to see her." I nodded and promised that I would. "Also, there's not an easy way to say this," he said, although he had clearly been thinking about how he was going to say whatever it was for a while now. "Please don't tell her that you and Penelope have split up. She really liked that girl and I don't want her to be spending the last days of her life thinking about you."

I nodded. "That's ok dad", I said, "I don't want her to worry about me either."

He smiled, "thank you", he said, "and another thing, I don't know what's wrong with you, but can you please make sure that you pull yourself together before we visit?" I nodded. He looked at me with considerate eyes, he had something on the tip of his tongue that was threatening to roll off and alter the afternoon's emotional equilibrium. "You do know that if there's anything that's bothering you then I'm here" he said. I smiled, he looked like he was about to say something else, but then he thought better of it and stopped himself. It was an unusual moment so we both went out of our way to avoid making any eye contact.

Whatever he was thinking would just go down as another one of those things that would remain unsaid. Instead of dwelling on it I changed the subject because I didn't want to risk upsetting things by letting the conversation stray into poignant territory.

"So what have you done with the garden since I was last here?" I asked. Then he smiled and took me outside to show me what he had done about the weeds that had dominated my last visit.

Chapter 6

It was only a few days after I was spiked that I laid down the first plank of my love rectangle by having sex with Sophie. Was it classy? No. Was it romantic? No. Was it at all smart? 100% definitely not. It was an absolutely stupid thing to do, and in the long run it really messed everything up for me. But at the time I couldn't help it because doing it was just too easy. In fact when she came into my office that day I knew right away that I was doomed and that it would be far too hard for me to resist. It wasn't even sex in the mainstream sense of the word, it was far cruder that that. It was carnal in nature and it was so clichéd and silly that it bordered on ridiculous. It was like something that was taken straight out of the FHM list of fantasies, but at the time none of that mattered.

Even if the idea had been a good one then the timing was made horrendous by the fact that she had recently been promoted to being Colin's 'staff liaison manager', so it really jeopardised my working life. The problem with any sex is that if it's not mutual then it means nothing, and if it means different things to both participants then it confuses everything. This confused everything. If it hadn't happened then I don't know where I would be now, but I'll bet that I would never have been fired, I would never have found myself waking up in a field stinking of wine and I would never have spent a night locked up in a Brighton prison.

***

I have to stress that at that point she was a virtual stranger, until then I had barely spoken to her beyond the formalities of everyday niceties. She had always seemed nice enough, but she was also a very private person so none of us really knew anything about her. I have no idea if she had ever liked me before then; to be honest I was actually pretty surprised that she even bothered to speak to me. I was hard to notice on account of the fact that I had always been competent enough to work without supervision and I was never good enough or passionate enough for her to have ever seen me as a rival or a power threat.

When it happened I was only a couple of hours into a very dull day and I was nursing a Merlot induced hangover while I contributed to the collapse of the world's economy from the comfort of my computer. It had been an extremely quiet morning and I had The Beastie Boys playing as loudly as the tiny speakers on my computer would allow. All the while I was dreaming up elaborate plans and fantasising about what it would be like to bring down western capitalism with my ideology as opposed to my apathy. If our civilisation ever collapses then I can guarantee that it won't be because of any protest or revolution - it'll be because there are far too many people like me who work in banks and don't pay enough attention to what we're doing.

As she walked in I was a perfect picture of idleness; I was twiddling my thumbs while my feet were on my desk and my shoes were off, meanwhile I was chatting to people on Facebook. "What the hell is this awful noise?" she asked with a bemused bark.

"Good morning Sophie," I responded while I closed my internet browser and tried to look enthusiastic and attentive, "it's the Beastie Boys. Do you want me to turn it down?"

"Who the hell are the Beastie Boys?" she asked, "and since when did you start listening to this kind of black stuff?" I shrugged and decided not to bother correcting her with the fact that all of the Beastie Boys are white.

Then my short sighted epiphany happened.

BOOM! I looked up and for a few seconds it felt like the world had stopped. I was amazed, it could have been the hangover talking, but I had worked with her for more than two years and this was the first time I had ever noticed how sexy she was. She noticed how I was looking at her straight away, and she smiled back mischievously, she knew exactly what I was thinking, and she liked it. She closed my door behind her and crossed the room. She milked the moment as she kept her eyes on me while she slowly lowered herself down onto the chair on the other side of my desk. She looked amazing; her tight white blouse emphasised her heaving cleavage and her navy pencil skirt looked so short that it was practically redundant. "And since when did you start coming in looking so unkempt and unsightly?" she asked with her seductive smile.

I reclined in my chair, by this point I was a lost cause - my eyes and my mind had strayed from the lifeless stock markets and were firmly fixed on her. I looked her up and down, like she was a centrefold pin-up and then all of a sudden my mind crystallised and her appeal became incredibly obvious. I really hate myself for saying this, but her appeal was that she didn't seem real. She seemed like the kind of girl that you only expect to see in films and magazines; she was carefree, she was easy and she fulfilled every single male stereotype of dead eyed female promiscuity. It was no wonder that she had climbed the corporate ladder so quickly, she was tailor made for a chauvinistic world.

I know that makes me sound like a bastard but the point is that we all do things that we're not proud of. In my defence it was her idea as much as mine, she had known exactly what was on my mind, that's why she had been consciously taking me over with every step. Then she walked behind me and slowly started to rub my tight pent-up shoulders. I tried my best not to enjoy it but her touch was electric and I could feel all of my anxiety draining as she captured what was left of my senses with her overpowering perfume. "What would Colin say?" I asked nervously.

"Forget about him," she responded softly, "mister big boss Director is practically impotent at the best of times." I had to smile; there was something so reassuring about the fact that Colin, with his two Jaguars, his fake tan and his six figure salary, had erection problems - for the first time ever I felt like I was better than my boss.

Then it happened. I knew that I was being an idiot, and in the back of my mind I kept picturing Janice telling me not to, but I genuinely couldn't help it. I tried to fight the urge, but something irreversible had gone off in my head and I simply had to do it. I kissed her, then she kissed me, and then predictably enough we had sex. Actually, it wasn't really sex, it was far tackier than that; at one point I even swept everything aside and threw her on to my desk. Despite the ridiculousness it felt fantastic; it was like a magical short-term anaesthetic that made everything temporarily insignificant.

***

With hindsight I can't begin to tell you how much I wish I had stopped it there and then, but I didn't. I don't deny that it was great, but it was also dangerous and it should have remained a one off event, but instead I let our assault on public decency continue for weeks. We may have started in my office but very soon we were using fictitious meetings as excuses to book out Executive meeting rooms for beautifully scenic, ego boosting, rendezvous on the 40th floor.

Although she was calling the shots I was more than happy to let her take me wherever she wanted. I wouldn't let myself instigate anything. Every time we met it had to be her idea and anything that happened had to be lead by her. In that sense our 'relationship' was an exact replication of our working relationship; she was in charge and I was subordinate to her every demand. I tried to tell myself otherwise, but I was overjoyed every time that she visited, and when I wasn't with her I was thinking about when I would next see her.

At the time I knew that I wasn't being me and in fact that was a large part of the attraction. I did it because I wanted to break free of who I was and I wanted to destroy every preconception and expectation that I had ever held of myself. I wanted to challenge my own self image by scrapping everything that I, and others, thought they knew about me and starting again. There were so many ways in which I could have reinvented myself, and if nothing else the fact that I couldn't think of a better way to do it is a damming scar on my imagination.

There were definitely whispers going around the office, but her position and the threat of cuts in the air made me feel safe from any social fallout; who could mock me when I was sleeping with the woman in charge of hiring and firing? I began to loosen up as I discovered the short term privileges that went with my position. I felt like I was bulletproof and that I had earned the right to walk with a swagger. For those few days I felt like a king. I no longer had to keep pretending to work every time she walked past my office, and I felt like I was able to stop paying attention to all of the rumours of redundancies.

Unfortunately it wasn't going to end well.

Chapter 7

Ironically the afternoon that I decided to break up with Penelope had been spent at a friend's wedding. It had been a really nice day; it was the kind of nostalgia ridden afternoon that feels like walking around in a living photograph album. It's only recently that I've started getting invited to weddings and christenings and the alike, and I love it. It's such a surreal feeling when you see the people you have grown up with starting to settle down and have families. It's like momentarily stepping into a time machine and finding out where everyone else ended up. Of course if you really cared about them then you would have stayed in touch, but all of that tends to be forgotten when you pull back your senses and move into an environment that's primed for rose-tinted reminiscing and remembering.

Ryan has always been one of my best friends. We've been friends for as long as I can remember; we went to school together, we obsessed over Morrissey and The Smiths together and we went to the same University where we studied accountancy together. As students we were practically joined at the hip, neither of us had many friends so we did almost everything together. When I learned to drive it was his dad that taught me, and it was my dad who taught him. I never really wanted to learn and nor did he, we've always hated the responsibility of driving, I know that cars can kill people, and so when I'm driving it feels too much like I'm walking down the road with a loaded gun or a whirring chainsaw. Ryan used to feel the same; there was a time when he was even more repressed and geeky than me, which made it all the more incredible that I was at his wedding.

It was only after graduation that we went separate ways – he did what everyone else I know seems to be doing and moved out to the countryside. Time changes everything and now he's become another one of those friends that I only ever see at weddings and reunions. At first he was relieved to be away from the pressures and stresses of the city, but within a few months he regretted his move. He found the countryside so boring and within weeks he was considering moving back, but any chance of it was torpedoed when he met another London escapee named Courtney. They got chatting one night in the village pub, then they had a few dates and within six months they were engaged.

***

The wedding itself was lovely. It was in a tranquil little church that was way out in the middle of nowhere, so in order to get there we had to get three different buses and ask a dozen strangers for directions, but it was worth it when we did. The atmosphere was great; the venue was spectacular, the scenery was stunning and the whole thing felt so natural because it was so obvious that they were meant to be together. It was also nice because I got to spend the evening chatting to old school friends and recounting all of the stupid things that we used to do. It was like reliving my childhood but without all of the shit bits.

One of the reassuring, but occasionally rather depressing, aspects of weddings and reunions is that you usually find that none of your former friends have managed to fulfil any of their dreams either. For example, Ryan had always wanted to be a policy wonk for the Labour Party. He used to preach long into the night about the wonders of socialism and the works of Marx and Engels, but now he's resigned his membership in despair of the last Labour government and he's become an administrative assistant for a rural bank. The most popular girls have all become secretaries rather than socialites, and the only one of us to ever get in the newspapers for anything was a quiet and reclusive guy called Jonathan Simmons, who was arrested for stalking a pop star. We had all gone to University with such high hopes, only for our grand ambitions to be retarded by world events. Some of us had excelled ourselves academically, but it turned out that we had worked hard and trained hard to prepare ourselves for a high-flying, fast moving, egalitarian, pre-crash world that no longer existed.

Everyone kept asking if I had ever finished the novel I had been writing while we were students. It wasn't anything special, and no I haven't finished it; it was about a group of 20 something's that had gone on a tour of Iraq and found themselves stranded in a desert. I had never really figured out what I was trying to say with it, and the lack of coherence dripped off every page. I had left it in a state of unfinished failure; I would forever wonder what it was that they had gone out there for and if they had ever found it. I knew that when they asked me they weren't really disappointed when I said no, they were secretly relived that I hadn't, if one of us had published a book then it would be a reminder that all of us could. Morrissey sang that we hate it when our friends become successful, and he was right, but it's not because we resent them, it's because we envy them. For example I would gladly read a million bestselling books, but unless I had written one too then I don't know if I could ever bring myself to read one that had been written by Steven or Janice; it would remind me that it could have been the other way around and that they should be reading about a group of people taking a spiritual journey around Baghdad.

Not everyone was doing so badly though, sadly the exception to the rule was Jarrod Smith. Jarrod is an obnoxious thug, and through nothing other than a combination of his own good luck and bad health in the family he had inherited a lottery-jackpot sized fortune and become an exceedingly slimy property tycoon. He even looked the part; his plus one was a busty blonde whose inappropriate dress could probably have been sold as lingerie. His face was moulded into a natural sneer and his tone underlined for me that he wasn't in the slightest bit grateful for his new found wealth and saw it as some form of just desserts for all of the hard work he'd put into achieving his hereditary privilege.

Despite our supposedly classless society Jarrod is living proof that the best way to achieve great wealth is to be born into it. Probably the nicest thing you could say about him is that he's consistent, in fact over the last 10 years he hasn't changed a bit. When I spoke to him I was almost surprised to find out that he's as much of a dick head now as he was back then. He came over, looked at me, then at Penelope and then back at me, then he leaned over and whispered in my ear "remember when we used to call you Pink Floyd? I always thought that you were a fucking fag."

***

After eating too much, drinking too much and dominating the dance floor I went out to the porch to get some air and have a smoke. The porch was well lit and it looked out across a gorgeous view of the mountains and the woods surrounding the hotel. I could still hear the band through the walls, they were very good and surprisingly versatile; they had combined all of the traditional wedding classics with some really obscure and fuzzy 1980s underground stuff that Ryan had requested. Their music weaved peacefully into the background while I lit up a cigarette.

I love cigarettes; they have such a welcoming, beautiful, and nostalgic taste. I came from a devoutly anti smoking family so I guess that makes me a born again smoker. I started because they gave me a way to establish my individuality, they let me rebel against my parents, albeit in the most unhealthy and conformist way possible. I know that this'll probably sound stupid but I don't ever want to give it up. I feel like we live in a socially detached age where almost everything we do is devalued and determined by things we have no control of, when you think about it like that then it feels like smoking is one of the few things we can do that we have any power over.

The cigarette was nice, but I had started to feel a bit removed from the evening. In its own way it had felt like a milestone. The reason I say that is because in its own way the wedding focused my mind on where my own life was going. It underlined how far away I was from achieving any of the things that I wanted to, whatever they were, and of course it concentrated my mind on the simple but terrifying question of whether or not I could imagine myself marrying Penelope.

It wasn't as if the idea was completely repellent, I want to be clear that there are a lot of far worse things I could have done than if I had married her - in fact I've already written about things I've done that are far worse, and there are plenty more to come. A couple of people at the wedding had already given me a well natured barracking and had been asking me how long it would be before I would be getting down on one knee. My stock response was to laugh it off, but after four years of us living together the pertinence of the question was obvious. After you have been together with someone for as long as we had then you can't help but wonder whether or not you have a future together. I'm a big fan of marriage and I fully intend to do it, I also want to have children too, but I only want to do these things once and do them with the right person.

I knew that she would probably have been getting asked the same friendly yet also rather personal and intrusive questions. One thing I will never know is whether or not she would have said yes if I had asked. Deep down I hope that she would have said no, but I also know that she loved me. I also know that she doesn't like confrontation and she hates disappointing people so I think that if she had been unsure then there's a very good chance that she would have felt pressurised into saying yes anyway. In my alternative reality I would give it three years before we divorced. I don't doubt that we would have had fun planning the wedding, and things would probably have been fine for a while afterwards, but I don't think that any elaborate fairytale wedding is enough to make a marriage successful if the two people simply aren't right for each other.

***

When we had first got together we were very different people from who we are now. She was a lonely and confused teenager, and so was I. We had come together through a shared love of Tori Amos, Oscar Wilde and not a lot else. At the time we were perfect for each other, we inspired each other to excel and we really helped one another to stretch out and reach beyond ourselves. For those magical first two years we had the sort of relationship that all of our friends envied and that my parents could only dream of.

It was after we graduated that things became different. Like every graduate I was faced with that all encompassing and life defining choice of either chasing my dreams or chasing some money. I thought about it for a long time, my instincts told me to get involved in student politics and use it as a step into charities and campaigns, but in the end I decided to prioritise my financial wellbeing, so I went to work in the City. BOOM! That was when the first cracks started to show. We argued about it a lot, she didn't really care enough about money and she wanted to leave London, she's not enough of a rat for the rat race and she didn't like the idea of me working the crazy hours that are meant to go with banking.

After a few weeks of an emotional stalemate we reached a compromise. We decided that we would do another few years in London so that we could make enough to pay off our loans and overdrafts etc. We never moved anywhere near the city centre though, instead we lived in a small one bedroom flat north of Highgate. She worked in a low stress administrative job much closer to home, while I got up early every morning and dragged myself onto the tube.

You can almost certainly tell exactly where this is going, it's such a familiar scenario and it almost always ends with an affair or a breakup. Needless to say, we started to drift; we were working in different parts of town so we made different groups of friends and we started doing our own things. We hardly ever saw each other, mainly because I always got back later than her and I needed to get up earlier, but even when we did we didn't have enough to talk about.

The alienation got to the point that we would go months without going anywhere special and even longer without having sex. She wanted to spend the weekends doing fun things and going on daytrips, but I was always so tired and drained that there wasn't even a small part of me that wanted to do anything other than spend my Saturday afternoons relaxing with the football. On top of that my Sundays were always reserved for reading a paper and then meeting with Steven and Janice so that we could talk about how shit everything was.

***

As we went home that night we both felt very happy about the wedding itself. The reception had been a lot of fun and we were both tipsy and well fed. I don't know what was on her mind while we sat together in the taxi holding hands. She leaned over and kissed me on the cheek. I turned round and gazed into her eyes, they were nice, friendly and warm, but that wasn't enough.

Chapter 8

Everything was about to go wrong. I didn't know it at the time, but whether you call it karma or coincidence then it was about to creep up on me and ruin everything. If my night of anonymous sex had been a case of temptation getting the better of me then Sophie was to prove one temptation too far.

It was a dark night outside and most of the others from my department were long gone. I was sitting at my desk watching the markets collapsing live on Bloomberg when she walked in with a scowl on her face. I waved to her and smiled as she sat on the chair across the desk from me. I didn't know what to say, so at first we looked blankly at each other, and then I raised my eye brows as if I was challenging her to cheer up. She rolled her eyes and shook her head as if to say that it was no good, then she reclined back in the chair and put her feet up on my desk and gazed out of the window.

"It's late, why are you still here?" she eventually asked.

I thought about what I should say. In reality it was because I had been waiting on the off chance that she might finish early and then we could hang out. But I didn't want to tell her that because it would make me sound desperate. "No reason. I've been working late" I said.

She nodded and exhaled, "me too" she sighed. There was a thick silence. I tried to avoid meeting her eyes, but they were too big and too vacant for me to ignore. I knew that she wanted to talk so I turned off my monitor, crossed my legs and turned to face her.

"Are you ok?" I eventually asked.

She smiled and sighed. Then she leaned forward and put her elbows on my desk and rested her head on her hands. "Yeah, I'm not bad. I'm just having a horrible day." I believed her; she looked like she was in need of a good stiff drink. I wanted to offer her a glass of wine, but she was still my boss so I didn't want to let her know that I kept alcohol below the desk.

"Is it anything you can elaborate on without violating HR policy?" I asked with just enough sarcasm to make it clear that I was concerned but I wasn't twisting her arm.

She giggled for a few seconds and then she sighed again, "It's just work", she said. "Central office has been kicking the hell out of us all day. They want us to pull out some kind of miracle recovery plan, that's despite the fact that they're cutting almost every single budget we have." She shook her head in regret of what she was saying, "And it's hard for the rest of us because they're demanding the impossible from Colin so obviously he's really stressed and he's taking it out on everyone else."

"You shouldn't be telling me this" I said convincingly. Even though I was only trying to cover my own back as an employee, just incase she attempted to use it against me one day in a tribunal.

"Why not?" She asked. "I know that you're good at keeping secrets so I trust you." She smiled, "besides, I haven't told anyone else, so if anything gets spread around then I know exactly who to blame." There was an awkward pause, "I could really do with a glass of wine" she said, "do you want one?"

"Sure thing" I said.

***

Although neither of us had said it we made the conscious decision to avoid the City bistros and go to a fairly downmarket old pub in Shoreditch so that we didn't risk seeing any of our colleagues. I knew about the rumours but they didn't bother me, what bothered me was if people thought that we were dating, because in my mind we weren't, this was the first time that we had even left the office together.

It was a shabby, dusty old man bar that we ended up in, it wasn't very nice and the clientele looked disinterested in life. We waded through the invisible sea of depression and ordered a bottle of mid price Merlot which she had paid for. After she poured it we exchanged unsure glances. "To better days" I said as I raised an impromptu toast.

"To better days" she responded as we clanged glasses. Then she took off her jacket, then she ran one of her hands through her hair and began to take a packet of cigarettes from her bag, then she put them back. I could see the flash of disappointment that ran through her mind as she remembered that we couldn't smoke in pubs anymore. She took out her Blackberry and put it on silent, "so how much can I tell you?" she asked, as if she was measuring my trustworthiness.

"You can tell me whatever you want" I said. "I won't tell anyone."

"How do I know that?" she asked.

"Because I haven't told anyone about anything else we've done together."

"Well you'd better not" she said with a snap. "Because I meant what I said. If you pass on anything I say tonight then you'll be fired." She sipped her wine, this was the first time she had ever referenced her seniority in front of me and I couldn't tell if she was joking or not. "Sorry about that", she said as soon as she realised how she sounded. "I'm just a bit stressed, I've been tired for days, and I've not slept properly for weeks." She sheepishly looked down to her wine and toyed with the glass for a few seconds. I didn't know what to say, so I didn't say anything, I just sat and listened as she pulled back the curtain and let me see behind the scenes and into her life.

"So what's going to be happening?" I asked, although my concern no longer had as much to do with her wellbeing as it did with protecting my job.

"I don't even know" she said, "and all they've told us is that they are sending us new targets in the next few weeks, which will mean more cuts."

"How much can we afford to lose?" I mumbled as I leaned forward.

"Well we've already frozen top level pay and made pretty big savings on procurement and energy costs, but that's barely made a dent."

She sipped from her wine and thought about if she was going to say anymore, then she peered at me through a small gap in her fringe. "It's just that it's only the start of the process and I'm already stressed out of my head." I nodded sympathetically as she tried to make eye contact. "Things are getting tough and I'm worried that I'm just not strong enough to be who they want me to be."

"I understand" I said softly.

"I'm not even a city girl", she said, "I'm not used to this sort of intensity. You know how if you look out to the countryside you always see those individual specks of light in the distance?" I nodded, "I grew up in a house like that. Before I moved to London I was one of those distant specks." She looked away and rubbed her eyes. We were silent for a few more moments. "Do people like me?" she asked.

"Yes" I said slightly hesitantly.

"No they don't, for example, why does Janice hate me?"

"She doesn't hate you."

"Yes she does."

"No she doesn't, she actually quite likes you."

"If she does then she has a funny way of showing it," she said flippantly. "Sometimes her tone can be so hostile that it's almost unreal."

We were silent for another intense moment as we both drank from our glasses. "I'm sure it'll all work out," I said in an attempt to fill the void.

"I hope so" she said, "because right now all I have to give the world is me, and that doesn't feel like a lot." She stretched her hand across the table for me to hold. I grabbed it tightly and relaxed my grip after a comforting squeeze. We didn't say anything else for a few minutes; we just looked away and used our free hands to drink our wine.

***

We shared a smoke as I walked her back home, it was a nice moment and I liked the feeling of her smooth hand rubbing against mine when she reached for the cigarette. She lived in a one bedroom flat that was only a few roads away from Liverpool Street Station and wasn't too far away from the pub. There was an awkward pause when we reached her front door. I had never been to her house before, so there wasn't a script or any fixed etiquette for moments like this. She shuffled forward and rested her head on my shoulder and put her arms around me. "Thank you so much for listening" she said, "I'm sorry to have put all of this on you, but I don't really have anyone else."

"That's OK" I said, "Any time", I kissed her on the forehead and held her loosely.

"Do you want to stay over?" she mumbled into my shoulder.

I nodded. I was relieved as she pulled away from the embrace and we assumed our traditional roles as we looked over our shoulders and went inside.

I had never been to her house before so I was surprised by how small it was; I had always assumed that she made far more money than I did. She lived on the second floor of a dark dingy stairwell with a flickering light that looked like something out of a horror film. When we got in she gave me the short and sweet tour of a kitchen that was too small for the two of us to stand in, a lounge with damp patches and peeling wallpaper and a bedroom that was cosy if nothing else. Without saying much else I took off my clothes and we had really dissatisfying, uncomfortable and robotically obligatory sex. It felt necessary though, it gave us the confirmation that everything she had just said was just talk between friends and a mere prologue to us returning to normality and continuing our secret affair.

The next morning I got up early and made her a cup of tea. While I was making it I realised that I would be going to work in the same clothes as I had left in the night before. I reflected on the fact that I had just spent my first full night with my boss. As I pondered life's complexities it occurred to me that from this point onwards everything would be different.

Chapter 9

It was another Sunday night and we were gathered in a quiet bar in Hampstead, the wine was in full flow and the banter was as high brow and topical as ever.

"Apparently I'm intimidating" barked Steven, "How the fuck am I intimidating? Who the hell could possibly be intimidated by me?" Janice and I shrugged, although we were both trying to suppress our growing urge to giggle. "Apparently someone's complained because I shout too much, have they never been in an office environment before? Who the hell are these over sensitive fucking idiots and what right do they have to fuck up my review?"

"But you've passed so you're safe" said Janice, "and that's the main thing."

"The main thing" he began, "the main thing is that I'm not getting a fucking pay rise and I'm going to have all of those idiots watching my every move. They did exactly what you said they would do; they set me a bunch of targets that Gordon Gecko himself could never come close to reaching. How the hell am I meant to surpass a so called target that was set in 2004? 2004 was way before the shit hit the fan."

"So self pity aside," said Janice, "what's your plan?"

He shook his head, "I guess I'm in the same boat as everyone else. I'll try to keep my head down, put in some extra hours and then start looking for a new job."

"That's about where I am too" I said tokenistically, even though I knew that Sophie was overseeing my review so I would be fine.

"Anyway," he said, as he turned to Janice, "I don't really want to talk about it at the moment."

"That's ok."

"I've got a game" he said, "pretend for a minute that we're all living in some kind of parallel universe and that you have a boyfriend." She didn't look impressed with his opening gambit. He noticed, but rather than apologising he continued to dig himself into a verbal hole. "Anyway pretend that you do, and then pretend that he's cheating on you with someone else," now she looked even less amused. "Well if we say that your make believe boyfriend was cheating on you, then would you rather that he was cheating on you with someone who looked exactly the same as you in every single way, or would you rather that he was cheating on you with someone who looked completely different?" What an ingeniously insensitive question...

"Well," she began, "first of all thank you very much for making me feel even more single than I already am," she smirked sarcastically and then paused. "Actually, that's a really good question, how did you come up with it?" he shrugged. "I would probably rather that we looked nothing alike." She stopped for a second as she pondered whether or not to add the next part. "But it's not important because I would dump him straight after he told me."

"I didn't say that it was him who told you."

"Fuck off Steven."

"Can I ask why you would rather that your hypothetical boyfriend found you so unattractive that he would choose to sleep with someone who looked utterly nothing like you?"

She sipped her wine awkwardly, "because people can fix how they look on the outside but not who they are inside." She responded with enough sincerity to expose the vulnerability of someone who had obviously suspected previous boyfriends of cheating on her.

He smiled and nodded, he decided not to push the emotional envelope any further. "Ok Floyd, in the name of fantasy we'll say that you're still with Penelope," I glared at him. "Ok, instead we'll say that you're with someone else then, regardless it's the same question I'm asking you," he winked.

I was stumped; to be honest I could see a rational case for both answers. After giving the question probably slightly more thought than it deserved I concluded that on balance I would probably rather that it was with someone who looked exactly the same as me. "Probably with someone who's exactly the same," I answered, with some degree of confidence.

"Why?" he asked me in a manner that sounded a little bit too much like an interrogation for comfort.

"Because," I began thoughtfully, "because, that would suggest that if anything she wanted more of me. It would mean that she wouldn't be doing it because she didn't find me attractive."

"You're right," he said, "It would suggest that it's just your personality that she doesn't like." He paused, "either that or that you just aren't capable of fulfilling her sexually." He winked at me as I shook my head. "So would you break up with her?"

"Yeah, I probably would."

"What if she told you that she had taken a test and it said that she was expecting?"

"That wouldn't happen."

"Yeah but just say that it did. Would you still leave her?"

"No, of course I wouldn't."

"What if the baby wasn't yours?"

"Fuck off" I said shaking my head, "anyway, what would you do?" I asked.

"Well," he said, "I would have to say someone who's the exact opposite, that way he would have to be someone who's scrawny, weak, and incapable of giving her an orgasm. It would have to be someone like you Floyd." He winked at me again, "that way she would come back to me within minutes." He smiled gormlessly at the wit and superiority of his own answer. "So Janice," he said as he turned and directed conversation back to her again, "have you ever been the other woman before?"

She almost spat out her wine at the brashness of his question. "What? That's utterly none of your business." Steven arched his eyebrow and gave her a sceptical glare, "no, Steven, no I haven't."

He smiled slightly sadistically, "oh come on Janice, we both know that that's not true." she glared back at him as he raised his eyebrows suggestively.

"Yeah, ok I have," she said after a pause. "My ex boyfriend Stuart had a fiancée, but I want to be clear that I dumped him as soon as I found out."

"That's really strong and noble of you," he said. "And I take it that you felt so guilty afterwards that you told her all about it?"

"Of course not," she snapped. "Why would I do that?"

"You're right," he responded, "when you'd had your fun that was ok, why does she deserve to know what he's been doing? Why does she deserve to know that he might even be doing it with multiple people, and getting all sorts of diseases while he's at it?" Now the tone was really intense, in a misjudged attempt at reconciliation he winked at her yet again.

"I hate you sometime," she retorted. "You have no right to get all proud and mighty about that sort of thing." She had taken the moralistic bait, "If I was a guy you would probably be encouraging me, or at least giving me a high five. What is it that you keep on saying? Men age like wine and women age like cheese?"

"Nonsense", he said as he smirked at his own joke. "You're about to go into all of that rubbish about how there's a double standard because if a man sleeps around then he's a stud and if a woman does then she's a whore etc, it's a feminist myth and nobody ever really says it. For what it's worth I blame the guy with the wife, I don't really care about 'the other woman', but you clearly do."

"That's crap Steven", she practically shouted, "It's a major double standard. All too often women are patronised and treated like we're incapable..."

"No you're not," he interrupted in a flippant manner that actually supported her point. "I know all sorts of extremely capable women. A double standard is like how when an old lady drops a tray of food everyone feels sorry for her and gathers round to help her out, yet if I did it then people would probably look at me like I was retarded. That's a double standard, what you were talking about is just an urban myth." He paused for breath. I considered intervening but thought better not to. She was right though, there's definitely a major social dividend to being a male; we get paid more, get promoted more regularly and have to prove ourselves far less, society doesn't expect so much from us so we can get away with not looking after ourselves and we don't have to worry so much about such frivolous things as makeup and dress sizes. "What about you Floyd, what's the worst thing you've ever done?"

During their argument I had faded into the background, but now even people at the other tables were looking curiously about what I might say – when you bear in mind what they had already heard then they probably assumed that we were all mad. I thought about it, all things considered it probably wasn't the best time to drop the Sophie-bomb. "To be honest I've not really done a lot, it was probably just the other week when you spiked me and I escaped out that poor girl's bedroom window."

"That can't actually be it," he said with his jaw dropped at my sheer prudishness.

"I'm afraid so", I said pretty meekly. "Aside from that I've always been pretty decent. I suppose I once got caught shoplifting as a teenager, but I don't think that really counts." He laughed and mock high- fived me. "So what's the worst thing you've ever done?" I dreaded what his answer might be as soon as I asked.

"I don't really know," he said contemplatively. "I got expelled from military school for fighting too much, which was ironic. I was also arrested for possession of drugs, but I got let off because the copper in question enjoyed a smoke" he laughed nostalgically. "I also once snorted a line with some friends and then spent the night out on the piss with some tramps, it was a crazy night and I woke up in a dole queue in Peckham minus my wallet, my keys and my dignity. But despite that I'm actually far tamer than most people think."

Sometimes it can be so hard to know when he's telling the truth and when he's bullshitting. If all of his stories are to be believed then he's beaten up almost every guy in London, been drunk in every pub in Britain and slept with almost every girl in Western Europe. Sometimes his stories contradict each other, and sometimes they make absolutely no sense to begin with. I didn't really want to dwell on his supposed innocence for much longer, so I went to the bar and got us another bottle.

When I got back the conversation had changed, Janice was midway through telling him that she was still thinking seriously about leaving London. "I know that I keep saying it, but this time I'm actually going to do something about it." The problem was that she sounded just as convincing as she had the last 20 times we had gone through the exact same conversation.

"No you won't," Steven said confidently, "you won't leave London because despite what you may say you secretly love this place. You thrive off the pressure of the City, and you'll get far too bored if you move anywhere smaller." She shook her head. "I am willing to bet that you're here for at least another year," he said.

"I really hope that I'm not. If I am then I'll be very upset." She poured us three new glasses. "These are supposed to be the best days of our lives and can any of us say we're really happy. Yesterday I was reading the paper and it said that a gang down the road from me had tipped an old man out of his wheelchair, taken his wallet and left him in the rain. I don't want to live in a city like that anymore. I just want to be somewhere else, anywhere else. I want to be in somewhere quieter, somewhere smaller and somewhere less arrogant and in your face."

Steven resisted the urge to chip in and tell her one of the thousand reasons why he thought she was wrong. Instead he just shook his head and poured some wine.

"So why not make it happen?" I said. "You keep talking about it but it's the same things you've been saying for years. If you really want to you can escape at any time, you've worked for a FTSE 100 company and you'll get picked up in an instant."

"Oh believe me when I say that I'm trying" she said as she drank from her glass. "If I'm still here in six months then I'm going to quit work and emigrate."

"I'll hold you to that. What about you Steven?" I asked, "How long do you see yourself being here?"

He shrugged, "where else is there? The rest of Britain is just as screwed up as us, only their shops aren't as good and their air is slightly cleaner. No matter where you go you will only ever find the same dammed problems. The only substantial difference between London and every other city in the country is that London is much bigger."

"Sadly I think you're right. You know that some day in the far and distant future our grandchildren will look back on this as some kind of golden age" I said, "and isn't that the most depressing thought in the world?" Steven nodded and Janice laughed. "It's quite funny, the world has infinite wealth and enough resources for seven billion people, and yet none of us ever have any money. Also, we're the first generation to have the ability to travel wherever we want in the world, and yet here we are in a claustrophobic little pub in London complaining about how awful everything is."

Janice nodded, "the big question is how many other trios are sitting in pubs around the world having almost identical conversations?"

And then there was Venus...

Chapter 10

And then there was Venus...

She was a ticking time bomb of emotions and she would ultimately leave me wrecked and humiliated in the middle of nowhere, but at that moment she was the epitome of everything that I had ever looked for in another person. She entered my life like in a momentary lapse of reason and had an impact that was akin to ecstasy.

That's not how the day began though, the day actually started just like any other. It began with the same early morning rise, the same battle to get on to the same overcrowded tube, the same inevitable delays, the same mobs pouring out of the same station and the same long wait for an elevator. When I eventually got up to my office I was already too tired and stressed to even think about doing any work.

One of the worst things about my office is that it's 19 floors off the ground. At first this seems like a really good thing; you get great views over London, and on a sunny day you can see for miles and miles. But after you've been looking at the same great view for more than a few months the feeling of freedom starts to dissolve. Instead you start to focus on the fact that there's a big wide world out there, and you can't get to any of it because you're trapped in an office. The view from my desk is particularly picturesque; it looks like it's been taken straight from one big Floyd mocking postcard. It stretches all the way down the Thames and tortures my eyes with tempting visions of the Southbank, the London Eye and almost every other tourist attraction that the city has to offer.

The office itself is institutionally joyless and looks and feels exactly the same as every other office in the building. It feels sterile and anonymous and we aren't allowed to improve it by bringing in photos, posters or any other symbols of our individuality.

I began the day by talking to George, who was at the end of an overnight shift. George was one of our cleaners, I always saw him first thing in the morning, and over the course of the last year I had built up a bit of a rapport with him. He was a really nice guy, he was genuine, honest and decent, but he was a picture of tragedy. He was the same age as me but he was almost twice my weight. I felt sorry for him because he was short, stumpy and fat and he had a bad ankle that made him waddle like a penguin. His designated area was my floor so he was always a background actor in my day to day life, but eventually one day we talked beyond our compulsory good morning mumbles. He had seen that I had a copy of The Great Gatsby on my desk and told me how much he loved it. I was very surprised because my inner snob would never have associated someone like him with classical literature. From there we started chatting, going for cigarettes together and lending each other books every few weeks.

Most of my books were pre war and most of his were postmodern, so our tastes were pretty complementary. We also exchanged music, I got him into things like The Smiths,

The Jam and the Pixies and he got me listening to more classical music.

I felt really sorry for him, even though I moaned about my job a lot I tried to be conscious of the fact that I was making more than double what he was, and I had a whole host of perks and benefits, like pension options and basic dental care, that he didn't. He didn't ever complain though, and he was more than happy to indulge my whining, especially if I repaid his attention with the odd cigarette and a coffee. He never asked me to pay but it was always implicit that it was expected, and if I suggested popping out for a cigarette at the end of his shift then it was only on the basis that I had some spares to go around.

I wasn't really in the mood for smoking at that point, so I suggested that we would catch up later in the week. As I watched him hobbling out I thought about how awful it would be to have nothing more than cleaning to look forward to. He told me that he had began cleaning his local pub when he was 16 and had been down on his knees ever since.

***

Most people naturally assume that the shaky economic situation would make people in the City work harder, but in my office it had the opposite effect. We were no longer chasing big bonuses or personal glories so none of us really cared anymore. The company was screwed and there was no single business transaction that could change that. There was an air of defeat about the building that resonated from top to bottom. The way that most of us saw it was that if our fortunes got much worse then either we would lose our jobs or the Government would be forced to step in and save us. We weren't experiencing mere turbulence, this was only the latest step in what had been a long drawn out decline. We had been financially stumbling for years, but now we were on the verge of falling into the gutter once and for all.

The board was pretty adamant that they needed to make cuts. Colin was up to his eye balls in stress, but that was because he made a lot of money and he was the sort of person that the deficit hawks would have loved to cut. In comparison I thought I was safe, but that wasn't just because I was having sex with my boss, it was also because I didn't think that I got paid enough to warrant them getting rid of me.

At that point it felt like the company was lying in a lonely hospital bed without any visitors or get well soon cards. Nobody was doing anything constructive and Colin was too busy trying to hold himself together to notice. He had short bursts of enthusiasm but they were so transparently desperate that I just wanted to hug him. No matter how hard he tried he couldn't help giving out signs of how broken everything was. One evening I saw him locked in a meeting room and wistfully browsing through an old scrap book of newspaper clippings from the glory days. He was such a contrast from the Colin that I had once known. When I joined the company he was a pillar of strength, but at that moment I felt like I was watching a miserable old man nostalgically studying an album full of glamorous ex lovers.

***

After a while I got up to get a coffee, we had run out it in the kitchen so I had to get it from the vending machine in the corridor. The coffee in the machine was absolutely vile, it was so thick, tarry and utterly disgusting. The problem is that I'm a coffee enthusiast, I truly adore it. A good cup of warm black coffee is a thing of wonder. If made properly it smells gorgeous, it looks divine and tastes like a small cup of heaven. The stuff from our machine tasted nothing like heaven, if anything it tasted more like Satan's urine. No matter how many cups I had I still winced every time I did as much as sip it. After having only half a cup I went downstairs so that I could have a cigarette to counteract the horrors of what I was drinking.

***

We weren't allowed to smoke in front of the building so I went out by the back exit. Hardly anyone went out that way except for George and the other cleaners, although that was because they weren't allowed to use the main entrance, so it felt like my own little concrete sanctuary. I took a short walk over to the regular step that I used for my breaks.

I sat down and put my 'coffee' to one side while I lit up a Marlboro. It was a nice day and I just wanted to spend it out there smoking, reading a book and passing time in the sunshine. My mind wandered as I temporarily allowed myself to zone out from everything.

By the time she came over I had lost myself in a calming vapour of nicotine. "Excuse me", she said, I turned round to see an astoundingly fresh beautiful face looking back at me. "Do you mind if I sit with you?" BOOM! I was instantly transfixed, she was stunning. She was petite, olive skinned and brunette, and she had a wonderfully spell-binding smile. She was fashionably dressed but she moved with such a curious sense of caution and a slight awkwardness that told me she was self conscious but down to earth. When she spoke she had a voice that was soft, expressive and just downright lovely. Every word that she said was beautifully expressed and pronounced to perfection, and every syllable made me want to hear more. I couldn't help but smile as I looked at her like a lovestruck puppy.

"Certainly", I responded after a few seconds of unintended silence. I shifted along the step as she smiled a big bright toothy smile and sat next to me. As well as being beautiful and well spoken she was carrying a half finished cup of unloved vending machine coffee, a Martin Amis novel and a half full packet of Marlboro cigarettes. I was instantly in love.

"I'm Venus", she said as she put her hand out, 'I'm new around here.'

"I'm Floyd", I responded as I reached out to shake it.

Chapter 11

I was captivated. She had an instant familiarity, she had that friendly and folksy kind of charm that leaves you feeling like you've been lifelong friends when it's really only been a few minutes. In time she would prove to be another step on my devastating road of self indulgence and self destruction, but in that moment nothing could have been further from my mind. It may only have been 10 minutes that we were together but they couldn't have been more ideal. Our conversation began with Martin Amis and touched on the history of literature, art, poetry and our views on almost everything else in the world except for our jobs. To be honest we could have been talking about the most boring financial transactions on Earth and it would have still felt like the world's most wonderful epiphany.

"So are you enjoying it?" I asked as I glanced towards her book.

"It's not bad" she said, "it's a bit downbeat in places and it's a bit pretentious, but I suppose that's what you expect when you read Martin Amis."

"Amen to that" I said, "Although I've just finished London Fields, which was excellent."

"Ooh I liked that one" she said as she sat down.

That was how we started. It may be a bit geeky but a love of literature and art is a pretty healthy building block for a relationship.

When we finished our cigarettes we turned to go back inside. "I wish we didn't have to go back to work" she said with a slight yawn, "I've enjoyed this nicotine break."

I nodded, "we should do it again sometime."

"Yeah, let me know the next time you need a smoke" she said with a friendly smile.

We said our goodbyes and went our separate ways when we got to the foyer, it turned out that she was one of the number crunchers on the bottom floors. As I crossed the room to go to the elevator I felt like I had been reborn. I had a new spring in my step and for the first time in weeks I felt good about myself. For all I knew she may not have seen it as anything more than a nice 10 minute chat, but in my hysterical hyperbolic state it felt like an important and irreversible conversation had just taken place and that I was in love. I knew that I didn't want to give her the chance to become just another one of the thousands of nameless people who swarm around our building. With that in mind the first thing I did when I got back to my office was look her up on Facebook and send her a friend request.

By the time I had got back upstairs a new tub of coffee had made its way to the kitchen, which lead me to believe that the crappy one that driven me into the arms of Venus must have been fate. I sat back at my desk and felt like a king; all things considered I was pretty satisfied with my morning. I happily sipped from a freshly poured coffee and watched Facebook out of the corner of my eye. Every few seconds I pressed refresh, I was trying not to focus too much of my attention on my computer screen, but inside I was pleading for it to tell me that she had accepted my request.

While I was waiting I heard the clicking sound of Sophie's heels as she approached from the other end of the corridor. If it had been a mere 20 minutes earlier then I would have gladly stayed, but I was too busy letting my mind get carried away with Venus, so I decided to do the mature thing and hide. The sounds of her heels were like jackboots getting steadily closer. I knew that if she saw me then it would wreck everything, so I ran out of my office and into Janice's.

Janice usually worked a lot harder than I did, but that morning even she was slacking, her jacket was in an untidy heap on the floor and she was barely even awake when I wandered in. She smiled lethargically as I let out a purposefully loud cough, then she flicked her hair out of her eyes and dragged her unconscious gaze from her computer. "Good morning" she said flatly. There was a pause as she noticed that I was grinning at her, "it's a Monday", she groaned, "Why do you look so happy?"

"Good morning", I responded with an idiotic smile, "I think that I may have just met the most perfect girl in the entire world." She rolled her eyes and slouched back in her chair, and then she adjusted her hair again and looked at me like I had grown a second head. "Her name's Venus", I replied without being asked. "And she's absolutely lovely. I just met her outside when I was sitting at the smoking step by the wheelie bins."

"What sort of name is Venus?" she asked with a hint of doubt in her tone.

"It's wonderful isn't it?"

She looked at me skeptically. "It's memorable", she said. Then she rubbed her eyes and gulped from a cup of vending machine coffee. "I just want to know how she gets the gift of a flamboyant and unforgettable name like Venus and I get stuck with a boring, crusty old one like Janice? If I ever get beaten to a job by a girl with a standout name like hers then it'll just have to be another one of the numerous things that I hold against my mother."

"My name's not much better," I said "can you imagine how annoying it is to share it with a 1970s rock band?"

"I can't imagine that it's much fun."

"It's awful" I said, "I don't even like Pink Floyd, I tried listening to them once, but they were a bit too avant-garde for me."

"Anyway", she said, "while you've been out seducing girls next to the wheelie-bins I've been deleting all of my dating profiles and erasing some desperately cringe inducing emails." She shook her head as she thought about whatever was in them. "I also tried to get some work done but I had about 10 clients in a row hang up on me because they're even more screwed than we are. It was all over pretty quickly so I've been watching the clock and spending my time answering the all important question of how many multinational corporate names come up on my predictive text."

"Any shock results?" I asked.

"Not really," she responded, "Starbucks, Coca-Cola, Microsoft, Hitachi, Vodafone McDonalds, and Sony all do, but Pepsi don't."

"That's cool" I said, although really I wanted to talk about Venus again. "On another note, I think that I might ask her out, what do you think?" I asked.

"I think that you've only just broke up with Penelope..." she said sarcastically.

"It'll be fine", I said with far too much confidence. "I've just added her to my Facebook" I said matter-of-factly.

"Oh right," she said curiously, "you're never really friends with someone until you're connected to them on at least one social networking system. So has she accepted yet?"

"Not yet. But when she does I'll show you pictures, she's beautiful."

"I'm sure she is, but is she single?"

"She didn't say that she wasn't" I said optimistically. She gave me one of those 'don't be so naive' looks and got back to working.

***

When I got back to my desk I logged on to Facebook and tried to think of a witty status I could put up. I wanted her first impression of the online version of me to be that I was suave, funny, sophisticated and humble. I wanted to think of a line that was so indisputably well thought through that it could tick all of these boxes and wouldn't instantly be followed by Steven calling me a Gaylord.

My past 10 statuses weren't very good, they were a mixture of Woody Allen quotes and Morrissey lyrics, and none of them made me look very cool. Over the next few minutes I put a lot of thought into it, but I couldn't think of anything. I kept almost putting up more witless one-liners or camp 1980s pop references, but thankfully my self control got the better of me.

Finally, after about 15 minutes I was still thinking, but my page refreshed itself with a short, simple and wonderful message; 'you are now friends with Venus Morgan.'

Chapter 12

A few days later I was sitting in a cold waiting room with Steven. I was nervous and awkward, but he was more comfortable and was acting like he was among friends – it felt like he was already on first name terms with most of the nurses. As I watched his care-free banter I wondered how he could feel so relaxed, I couldn't possibly be so calm; unlike him I had never undergone a Chlamydia test before...

I probably didn't need to go, but I was there because I was cautious. I still felt uneasy about that unknown one night stand, and by that point I had heard far too many rumours about Sophie to be entirely comfortable. I know it's stupid but we had never bothered to use a condom because she was on the pill, but according to the water cooler everyone knew someone who had been with her and nobody said that she was particularly safety conscious. I wasn't only there because I was cautious, I was also there because I was being presumptuous and I thought that if there was any chance whatsoever of anything even possibly happening with Venus then I wanted to make sure that I was ok. In contrast with my curious combination of caution and optimism Steven was there because he was reckless.

I wasn't looking forward to having to pee in the jar. I can't make myself do it in front of other people; I even find myself getting nervous every time I pee at a urinal. I can be at bursting point, but as soon as someone else is in the room my stage fright takes over and I find it impossible to even begin. It seems like every time we're out anywhere Steven always goes to the toilet at the exact same time as I do, and I'm pretty sure he does it on purpose. He almost always goes for the urinal right next to mine and unsubtly sneaks a peek as if to reassure him that he's still bigger than me.

He kept looking at his watch impatiently, we had only been there for 10 minutes and he was already starting to get bored. He looked around the waiting room before leaning closer and muttering to me about work. He had felt emasculated earlier that day because Colin had put him down in a meeting in front of other colleagues and a company partner. Apparently Steven had questioned one of his projections and Colin had dismissed him by calling him an amateur blogger and a wannabe economist. I knew that it had hurt him; Steven had always believed that he and Colin shared an almost master and apprentice like bond and now he was finally starting to realise that actually all of Colin's friendships were superficial and plastic. "The way he said it was just so rude, it was as if he wanted me to feel utterly useless." I felt quite bad for him, he had always cared far too much about impressing people who simply didn't care about him unless he was making them money.

"Don't worry, he's like that with everybody" I said. "Besides, there's more to life than impressing people like him. And anyway if he didn't like you then he would never have invited you to the meeting in the first place would he? He's never invited me into anything like that."

"I guess not" he said slightly more positively. "This is all such a waste of time" he added so that he could change the subject.

"There is not even a single part of me that really believes I have anything, I just want to get out. It's a good thing I don't have tits or they would have fallen off from boredom by now. We've been at work all day and I've got far too much to do to be spending my time in a place like this." I couldn't be so blasé, I was still in shock; I had always presumed that I would die without ever having to visit a GUM clinic.

"Do you ever feel like sometimes you should slow things down?" I eventually asked him.

He shrugged, "it depends what you mean by slow things down."

"I mean all of the hard drinking and all of the girls. Is it really worth it?"

"Yeah it is," he said very deliberately. Then he paused, "everything I have ever done has been my choice and I don't regret any of it. There have been a few incidents along the way, but I don't want to die wishing that I had done more. Think of how many millions of people die every year wishing that they had spent less time at work and more time living. For all I know I could be hit by a bus tomorrow. You must have heard the phrase that it's better to regret something you did than something you didn't, well that's my philosophy."

"I think I had grown out of that mindset by the time I left school" I said dismissively.

"I didn't" he said with a slight hostility in his voice. "When I go out I take the attitude that I don't know what's going to happen after tonight, and I don't want to either. Our whole generation lives for the weekend because there's not a lot else. It's not about self destruction and it's not that I don't care about what happens to me, but it's because I want to feel like every moment I have is a privilege."

"But how can you live like that?" I asked. "I've only been doing it for a few weeks and I'm already exhausted."

He shook his head slowly, "I don't live like that. I may enjoy a drink or two, but I've never been late for work, I've never missed a deadline and I've never even cancelled on you or Janice."

"But you're intoxicated five nights a week and that can't be good for you. I like you but I worry about you, you're the target market of all of those public health campaigns."

"I appreciate your condescending concerns but I'm not retarded or anything. You guys may not believe me when I say it, but I can quit all of this any time I want. I don't need to drink or take pills or anything like that, but I like them." He put his phone away and carried on, "So yeah ok I've definitely done some pretty stupid things, but no one has ever coerced me into anything, and when I've made my choices I've known fine well that sometimes I'll end up with a sore head, and heaven forbid I may even end up in here." It was his turn to ask me a question. "What the hell is it with you anyway? Why do you always feel like you need to be apologising for something?"

"I don't know," I said, "I guess that it's just because I feel like I still owe Penelope an apology for everything that's happened." I was slightly surprised, I felt like I was on the verge of having one of my first ever heart to hearts with Steven. "It's just that amidst it all I feel like I'm not really being me anymore."

"No offence," he said, which instantly alerted me to the offence he was undoubtedly about to cause, "but that's the best thing about all of this. It's not you, and that's why you're so confused by it all. You're not really in any sort of crisis," he did that annoying quotations thing with his fingers when he said crisis, "you're just in a moment and you're living through it. It'll pass pretty quickly and then afterwards you'll wonder why you ever got so worried in the first place. I can guarantee you now that you won't still be pining after her when you're 40. In fact I bet that by the time we're 40 we'll both be just like everybody else, we'll have families we resent, cars that costs far too much and mortgages that are threatening to bankrupt us."

"All of that may be true," I responded, "but right now all that I can think about is the fact that I might have an STD."

He sighed, "Sex is sex, and everyone worries about the clap at some point. But at least you're actually having sex, because there are a lot of people who aren't even doing that. What about that cleaner you hang out with, he's so fat he can't even see his dick, what are the odds anyone else has?"

"Leave him out of this."

"Why, is he your boyfriend?"

"That's a really original comeback."

There was a silence. "I've got a question for you", he said, "would you rather be straight and have to be celibate for the rest of your life or would you rather be gay and have all the men you could ever dream of whenever you want them?"

I was perplexed, "probably gay so that I could have it whenever I wanted. A lifetime of celibacy would be quite stale."

"Yeah but you could only be with men."

"But if I was gay then that surely wouldn't be a problem."

He gave me a look that suggested I had just been coming on to him. "I always knew you were a bit of a fag but you're usually more subtle about it than that."

"What would you do then?" I asked.

"No sex of course, I don't like men."

Our debate was interrupted when he got called away for his date with the jar, which left me alone and very worried. I looked around, no one else in the waiting room was making any eye contact; they all had their heads down so they could seem anonymous, all that I could hear was the turning of magazine pages. It felt like an eternity before I was eventually called away.

When I went in to the nurse's room I was terrified about what could happen. The nurse was about as unfriendly as it's possible for someone in a caring profession to be. She seemed cold and disinterested, she verbally scolded me for being there in the first place and she practically threw a cup at me to pee in. I thought that she was just going to stare at me, but thankfully she left the room for a minute or two before she came back in smelling of cigarettes.

***

When I saw Steven again he was talking to a girl by the reception desk. She looked really good, she didn't look at all like the kind of girl you would expect to meet at a GUM clinic; she was tall, blonde, olive skinned and busty, and she had the kind of contagious laugh that reverberated around the room. "Hey Floyd," he said, "this is Willow; she's also here with a friend." He turned to her, "this is Floyd. I'm here to keep him company. He's worried he might have caught something from his boyfriend." He turned back and winked at me. I grinned like a gargoyle and tried to pretend that none of it was really happening.

***

A few days later my results came back and they were clean, which on one hand was great, although on the other I was actually slightly disappointed because it meant I had gone for nothing. It was a Saturday afternoon and I was sitting around at home, I was bored out of my mind. I tried to watch TV but there was nothing on, I had thought about browsing a book, but there was nothing that I could actually be bothered to read. I knew exactly what I wanted to do; I wanted to go and see Venus, but I still hadn't plucked up the courage to ask her out yet. I thought about emailing her but I didn't know what to say. I kept logging on to Facebook to see if she was available, but she was never online. I had a missed call from Sophie but I didn't want to call her back in case I ended up sleeping with her again.

I decided that I wanted to do the responsible thing, so I called Janice, who I knew wouldn't let me do anything too stupid, but she was too busy with other things. Her rejection made me sense that God was telling me to go out and get drunk, so I called Steven, who was clearly still in bed when he answered.

"Hey Floyd," he yawned "How are you doing?"

"I'm not bad. The test came back clean so I was thinking about celebrating."

He laughed, "That's good news. So what do you have in mind?"

"Nothing special," I replied, "I'm just bored and I was thinking about heading to the pub, fancy joining me?"

"I don't know about that," he said, "I'm kind of busy right now." As soon as he said it I heard a girl giggling in the background.

"Steven, is that a girl with you?"

"Yeah, you remember Willow don't you?"

"Is that the same Willow that we met at the GUM clinic?"

"Yeah, that's the one."

"Have your results come back yet?"

"Not yet, but don't worry about it, she's on the pill, so I'm playing it safe."

"Playing it safe? Does she know that you're still waiting for results from a Chlamydia screening?"

"Of course not, why would I tell her something like that?"

"Because you might have it…"

114

"If I have it then I'll just take a pill and get rid of it. Besides when I think about it I'm almost certainly clean."

"Let's just hope you are. Are you at least wearing a condom?"

"Unfortunately yes"

"Good, I'm glad you're taking precautions."

"I don't have anything, just chill out. I'll see you tomorrow."

"Don't say I didn't warn you, I'll see you tomorrow."

***

For the rest of the day I felt really lonely. I nearly ended up going round to see Sophie, but I somehow managed to stop myself. It was very close though, I even went as far as going for a walk, in which I 'accidentally' passed her house.

Regardless of my own ineptitude I considered it to be an achievement that I went to bed by myself that night. I had just gone a whole week without getting drunk or having sex with her, it was hardly heroic but it was a start.

Chapter 13

Now that I was forcing myself to go cold turkey on the Sophie front it meant that I could concentrate all of my charms and efforts on my attempts to woo Venus. We had been getting on pretty well during our short cigarette breaks and our Facebook chats, so the early signs were good. A few days later we were in her office watching some anti capitalist protesters out the window. There were about 60 of them and their anti banking chants were getting quite aggressive, but we were safe enough because behind their bravado they were just a bunch of middle class students. Steven had gone out for a cigarette and a debate with one of them, which had been quite funny because rather than engaging with him the ringleader had kept shouting "money pig!" and "get your snout back in the trough" through a megaphone.

The police had sent out about 15 officers, all of whom were hanging around looking angry and brandishing weapons, but none of whom were going to use them for any purpose other than to cement the rituals of a stand-off. Colin had been given an advanced warning of the protest so he had made sure he was in the building before anyone else. He had been stuck in his office all day, for all of his boldness there must have been a part of him that wasn't happy about the fact that such a large portion of the public found him totally despicable. With the exception of Steven, who had flouted it, we had all been banned from going out via the front door in case one of the protesters attacked us. I really doubted that any of them were going to try anything, so I felt really stupid using the back exit when I went out for lunch.

Venus was looking almost admiringly at them; they had to be pretty fearless to be camped out bang in the heart of the Square Mile. I wanted to tell her an impressive story from my days of protesting, but there wasn't much to tell as none of the protests that I had been on had amounted to anything. It was certainly an odd backdrop for it, but I used that moment of rose tinted nostalgia and social breakdown to take the plunge of asking her if she wanted to 'do some sightseeing' over the weekend.

As soon as I asked her I saw a flash of what looked like it could have been either surprise or panic in her eyes. I braced myself for the worst and sheepishly looked at my feet. I felt rather pathetic, so I offered her the chance to use a get out of jail free card. "I mean if you're busy we can do it another time, there's no rush." She didn't respond straight away, I could feel my body going all prickly with worry as I worried that I had upset her, but then I slowly looked up and saw that she was smiling.

"I'm free" she said, "you don't need to make excuses for me, it sounds like fun." As soon as she said it a mix of excitement and terror quickly spread through my body. I had been thinking of asking her out for a long time, but I hadn't actually prepared myself for what I would say if she actually said yes.

I felt out of my depth and gulped, "where shall we go?"

She thought about it for a few seconds, "it's your choice" she said, "and then I can choose next time." My ears instantly picked up on her possibly mistaken use of the beautifully welcoming phrase 'next time'. I decided not to put anything in jeopardy by asking any follow-up questions which could potentially result in my rejection, instead I went back to my office to plan a date.

She had only been in London for a few months so I decided that it would be a good idea to stay in town and do the whole city centre thing. One of the good things about living in London is that there's never a shortage of things to do. If nothing else it's a city that lends itself well to those early dates when you're trying to get to know each other; it's like one big colourful conversational prop so it has something for everyone.

I had been getting missed calls from Sophie for a few days now. I didn't quite know what was happening, so I was still going out of my way to avoid her. I know that I should have been honest and told her that it was over, but at the time, and much to my regret, I had decided that I was only going to say anything if it looked like Operation Woo Venus was on course for success.

***

"It's so great to see you outside work" I said with a big rehearsed smile as I looked in the mirror. "You look wonderful" I tried to say with a slightly toothier one. Then it got really surreal as I started kissing my hand. I had already shaved, showered, gelled my hair, and applied far too much deodorant. I had also covered my chin in the strongest

118

aftershave that I could find, and had rubbed all sorts of metrosexual youth creams all over my face so that it smelt of a combination of trendy oils. I wanted to look much cooler than I really was, so I had put on my only Hugo Boss shirt with a pair of designer jeans and brogues. I was listening to Eminem and bouncing around the room while I put the finishing touches onto my semi-successful attempt at an overtly fashionable look.

I had been expecting the worst from the Underground, so I had got up really early and made sure that I left with plenty of time to spare. Unfortunately the service had been annoyingly efficient, so I had about 45 minutes to kill before meeting her. I decided to go to a small quiet side street cafe in Soho; it was the kind of place that businessmen went to between meetings and pimps went to when they wanted to find new clients. It wasn't bad though, and the coffee was nice enough, even if it wasn't going to win any awards. The mood was relaxed and the music was quiet alternative rock, but despite the calm setting I still had a nervous lump in my gut. I didn't know what to expect, I didn't even know if she considered it to be a date. I didn't want her to misread anything, so I knew that I had to be explicit about my intentions without coming across as strange, overbearing or scary. I wanted her to know in the least creepy and intense way possible that I liked her.

I tried to distract myself with a newspaper, but my attention span was nonexistent. The main story was about a dog that looked like John Lennon, so it was hardy earth-shattering stuff. It was while I was contemplating the decline and fall of British journalism that I had a sudden brainwave and decided that I was going to go out on a limb and ask her if we could begin our afternoon with a kiss. The rationale for my thinking was that it would be a good way of asserting that I was interested in her and that I wanted it to be a date. There was an obvious downside insofar as she might say no and then leave, but it was a risk I was willing to take.

After what felt like a long anxious eternity I eventually saw her approaching. She looked amazing; she was calm and relaxed, and the best part was that she didn't look like she was only there out of pity. She was bedazzling, in short she was a work of art. She looked as natural as it's possible to be in an age of cosmetics; her hair was flowing and beautiful and she was a picture of summery goodness. She was also better dressed than me; she was wearing a cute white beret, nylon flip-flops and a nice flowery dress that was hidden below a cute blue denim jacket. She finished her look with a big colourful badge that screamed COUNT YOUR BLESSINGS.

Unfortunately I was far from smooth. I was shaking with fear and my palms were already sweating as I stumbled and blurted my way through what was probably one of the scariest and worst constructed sentences that I had ever said. "I uh, I um, I want to kiss you". I eventually forced it out. My word choice was terrible; I hadn't even asked her if she wanted me to, I had only said that I was going to. I was shaking, but she smiled at me sympathetically in the same way that you would a lost child or a charity appeal.

"Ok", she said, "what if I give you a kiss on the cheek now, and if we have a nice afternoon I'll give you a proper one later." She smiled as I nodded, then I froze on the spot as she leaned in and kissed me on my cheek. Without wishing to sound like some kind of stalker I have to say that even her kiss was perfect, it was soft, it was gentle and it was divine. I just read that back and it's so utterly cringe-inducing, but it's also true, at the time the light press of her lips felt perfect.

***

After we left the cafe we walked through the narrow Soho streets and into the touristy glare of the West End. Soho's a good place to meet because it's central and it's convenient. It's a bit rough around the edges and a bit of a throwback but it's got lots of nice bars, restaurants, cafe's, book shops and gardens. During the day it's all fairly subdued and a bit cheap and tacky, but at night the area comes to life as the media types clock off for the day and the celebrities come out to play while the streets flourish like proud colourful peacocks.

The next stop on our magical mystery tour was Trafalgar Square, where we watched as thousands of tourists buzzed like flies around Nelson's column. We broke the ice by creating fictitious stories for the various characters that came and went. We sat on one of the benches that overlooked the square and began our fantasising. What if stranger number one was in London to meet his long lost grandparents? What if stranger number two had just won the lottery, but her prize was dependent on her not breaking cover? What if the suitcase stranger number three carried was full of ransom money? Or what if there was someone hiding inside it? These were the sorts of scenarios that raced through our heads and weaved their way into our conversations as we watched the city open up before us like a surreal scene from a holiday brochure.

Out of the corner of my eye I saw George waddling down the steps at the other end of the square. Venus didn't recognise him, but she pointed him out, "I feel so sorry for that man" she said as she looked over, "when do you think he last saw his feet?" As I saw him hobbling through the square I faked a laugh and turned my head, then I took Venus's hand and started walking away. At the time I felt a knot of regret, but I couldn't undo it because that would be even worse. I kept walking, I was literally praying to myself that he hadn't noticed me and if he had that he honestly thought that I hadn't noticed him. I knew that I was being inconsiderate and I didn't even know what I was scared of, but only a few minutes ago I had been feeling good about myself and I didn't want my fat friend to cramp my style.

As I lead her away we went through Whitehall where we took the usual photos next to the horses of the Household Cavalry and Westminster Abbey and Big Ben. The sun was shining as we crossed the Thames arm in arm and posed for more tastefully clichéd photos while we accidentally ruined lots of other people's. On the bridge I reached into my pocket and checked my phone, I didn't think that George had my mobile number, but that didn't stop me turning it onto silent in case he called. He didn't try so it wouldn't have mattered anyway, but that didn't stop me from telling myself that if I couldn't hear him then it was ok not to answer.

***

We walked past the London Eye and went for a riverside coffee, by that point I had calmed down again and we exchanged our life stories over something milky and warm. I wanted her to think I was really interesting, so I was a bit creative with the truth. I tried to make it out that I was some kind of culture vulture and attempted to paint myself as somewhat of an anti-authoritarian and political rebel. I told her the bits about my dad's frolicking and his sleaze, but I didn't sensationalise it with all of the mortifyingly scandalous details. I also didn't go into much detail about my quarter life crisis, instead I simply mentioned that I had recently broken up with someone and I didn't mention Sophie at all.

She told me all about herself; she had grown up in the kind of liberal, Guardian reading, middleclass household in the South of England that it's hard to struggle against. She was born into high expectations; her mother was an architect and her father was a scholar with a building named after him at Oxford. She had gone to a world famous private school and as the most minor form of middle class revolt she opted to study classics at Cambridge, but none of that could save her from Generation Debt. She had always wanted to work for an NGO or a charity, and she had spent months looking for the kind of good ethical jobs that you only ever see advertised in magazines like the New Statesman. But in the bad economic climate all of those jobs had dried up. By the time that she graduated she had never had a job, so after a lot of soul searching and naval gazing she took up evening classes at a local former polytechnic and developed her computer skills. She kept applying for the few liberal jobs that were coming up, but in an age where everyone who has a social conscience also has a 2.1 degree it was totally fruitless, and now she worked for the same soulless bankers as I did.

If working in the City had become a depressing convenience for me then it was a personal and ideological catastrophe for her. Unlike me she had actually been a proper teenage radical, and only a few years ago she had been smoking pot and marching and protesting against the same people who were now paying her wages. It wasn't all mainstream rebellion though; despite her super-privileged upbringing she tried to practice what she preached and even spent one summer living in a grotty commune with a group of activists who stole their food from skips and spent their afternoons talking about how they could change the world. Those days had been spent fighting against the global dominance of the war machine and trying to live outside the Babylon of modern capitalism. All of that was before the crash, and now the same counter-culture protesters are wither hedging their bets in the city or have gone back to being students. Working for someone big and powerful is a simple premise, but balancing her beliefs with this small scale contradiction threw her into her own quarter life crisis. She had only just reached the point of reconciling herself with an all too regular moral trade-off.

"Do you enjoy your job?" she asked, with a smattering of sadness in her eyes.

"Nobody does," I said, "I only tolerate it because it pays the bills and it used to be safe, that's about it."

"I don't think I can ever learn to tolerate it" she said, "I just feel so ground down every time I step out at the end of another monotonous day." I nodded in agreement, "it just feels so devoid of purpose and just so totally fucking empty" she said.

Her desperation was so familiar. I had seen it in so many other people, but there was something so naked and naive about hers. The proper grinding of the City was yet to set in, as I looked at her I knew that she would never be one of the people who stay in all night to clinch that last sale or fit in that least meeting, she saw it as a job rather than a lifestyle. I could tell exactly where she was headed, all of us head the same way, and there are three emotional stages that almost all new employees inevitably go through.

The first one is hope; this comes when you first walk into our marble foyer and you see all of the priceless art that adorns the walls and you're at the point where you buy into all of that corporate identity stuff. This is the point when you still dream about receiving the fruits of your labour and it's the short and significant time when you honestly believe that you're climbing a steady ladder that will lead you to success, comfort and wellbeing. This is the time when you turn up early, stay late and try in vain to befriend all of our bosses and your clients.

The second stage is one of apathy; this is when you realise that stage one is all bullshit and you resign yourself to being bored and constantly trying to find new and creative ways to get away with doing the bare minimum work. This is the point when your salary seems to stand still and you start to resent the system. So many of us fall at this mental hurdle and leave shortly after in order to try and follow an alternative path before it's too late. Meanwhile the rest of us stay indifferent, but at the same time we go out of our way to do just enough of the box ticking stuff to justify ourselves in appraisals and make sure that we pass all of our reviews.

The third and final stage is one of complete despair; this is when we realise that the lives we have fallen into bear no resemblance to the ones that we want. People in stage three can become removed and depressed, and many of us actively fantasise about what it would be like to march in one day with a shotgun and empty it over all of our clients one-by-one. I had been hopeful for a couple of months and I had been apathetic for a long time, so it had taken me almost a year to reach the third stage. However, Venus had always been so cynical that she managed to skip the part about hope, which suggested she was on course to reach stage three in record timing.

As the old clichés go, misery loves company and a friend in need is a friend indeed. It was with those well worn out phrases in my mind that I looked into her poor bewildered eyes and I realised that I wanted her to reach my stage as soon as possible.

Soon enough we were holding hands across the table and talking and reminiscing about our favourite books. She's a geek, like me; she loves The Pixies, Chuck Palahniuk and the Velvet Underground, she also likes watching reruns of Twin Peaks and enjoys nothing more than being wrapped up with a good hardback book. She painted a beautifully vivid image in my head of her sitting alone in a tough old armchair with a big thick chunky classic and a mug of hot chocolate while the sound of raindrops and thunderstorms from the outside drowned out the burning and crackling of her coal fire.

She said that she loves being inside and watching the rain. She loves the whipping patterns it makes on her window, but she also loves the sight of streams of rain forming and running down the gutters. She may have been a soft skinned southern girl but she told me that she looked forward to winter all year long. Her complexion may be benefited for the organic rays of the summer sun but she loved casting a glance upon a dark lonely night; for her sleet, snow and close-knit winters went together with coco, warmth, and companionship.

***

After we left the cafe we walked along the riverside. We passed a group of drunken buskers who were setting up on the patch of grass next to the Southbank Centre. They didn't look like they were going to be very good, and one of them was practically passed-out before they had even started. We had to dodge broken glass as we studied the subversive graffiti that peppered our route. All of the messages were stark and simple and captured the mixture of futility and cynicism that have defined Generation Debt. It was like reading a twisted socialist self-help book. One wall said 'DOWNSIZE YOUR DREAMS', another one proclaimed that 'A SPECTRE IS HAUNTING EUROPE' and another one simply read 'WE ARE A MEDICATED NATION'. After reading the graffiti we saw some of the street performers and mimes, and then we walked up to the roof garden on top of the National Theatre.

From there we shared some Pimms as we held hands again and finished the day by watching the sun melting into a cluster of buildings and the residential city centre cloak of smog. The orange lens pierced through the pollution and let the buildings cast their majestic shadows over the dark gray Thames.

"Thank you for a lovely day", I said with a nervous smile.

"Thank you," she said. There was a pregnant pause. "I think you've earned a proper kiss this time", she said, as she leaned in and gave me a light kiss on the lips.

***

If I could have magically stopped time at any point in my story then I would have done it there and then. That kiss was the highpoint of this story and one of the highpoints of my life to date. That kiss was the turning point and from here on in everything I did was a total mistake. I shouldn't even have let her kiss me. With hindsight I should have gone home, broken up with Sophie, got a new job and fled town.

All of these things would have been smart, sensible and forward thinking moves. Instead I went with the horrendously dangerous advice of trusting my instincts and following my heart (a lethal combination) and it left me unemployed, homeless, single and miserable.

Chapter 14

The next day I caught up with a mildly hung-over Steven to watch the football and have a couple of drinks. Janice was off doing something else so we went for a bromantic afternoon of one-upmanship and manly banter (aka manter). We both support Fulham, who were losing as usual, but it didn't matter because we were so used to them losing that we were practically immune to it. Despite the football I felt pretty good. I was still feeling light and breezy from my date, and I was looking forward to seeing her at work on Monday. I was also feeling assertive. I had slept on it and firmly decided that it was time for me to do something about Sophie, although by the time I woke up she had already texted to invite me round for the afternoon to 'hang out'.

We were sitting at a badly slanted table in a nice old fashioned pub just next to Camden Market. It was a weekend so the usual commotion was going on around us, but it was quite sunny outside, which meant that inside it was pretty quiet. We were drinking locally brewed ales and eating salty peanuts while I thoughtfully recounted almost every minute detail of my date to a very bored looking Steven.

"So here's the part I don't get", he said, "why did you take her to Soho? It's disgusting. If you're trying to impress a girl then you take her out in the real West End. You should have gone to some posh Mayfair bar to drink overpriced cocktails and eat oysters, or whatever people like you do on dates. Then you should have pottered around in Kensington and you could have done wine or something cultural. You shouldn't ever meet anyone you like in somewhere like Soho, it's alright for a pint but it's full of gays and tramps."

"Ok in some ways it probably wasn't the best place to start", I said, "but your views of it are pretty out of date. Soho's not too bad these days. Anyway it's comfortable enough and it made me look liberal, open minded and trendy, and most importantly it went well."

He scoffed into his pint, "pfft you say liberal like it's a good thing, nobody should ever respect a liberal. Personally I think that it would have made you look like even more of a queer."

I frowned, then I looked over each shoulder and leaned in as if I was about to share a closely guarded secret with him. "The best part is that it wasn't a one-off, we even have a second date planned."

"That's good," he said benevolently, and then he forced a smile, even though he couldn't have sounded any less happy for me. "I'm not trying to rain on your parade, it's just that sometimes you need to think about the messages that you're sending out. Everything is about building brand of Floyd and I hope Soho isn't it. Think about how much better it would have gone if you had taken her somewhere decent to start with. There would have been none of that Southbank nonsense and you could have been waking up next to her this morning."

"I doubt it" I said shaking my head at the very idea. "Anyway, even if by some miracle she had said yes then I think that we would have been rushing it somewhat, don't you? Anyway, whatever happened to your whole 'don't sleep with the people you work with' philosophy?"

"That rule only really applies to me", he responded. "I wouldn't be stupid enough to do it, but I don't really care about who you see as long as you're not moaning about your so called 'crisis' any longer." He paused and took a drink, and then he looked right at me and smiled mischievously, "It's just not a good idea though, especially not if you're also seeing your boss."

Suddenly I began to feel very panicky and my mind froze over with fear. He kept gawking at me, I knew from the distinct lack of any subtlety in his tone that he must have heard about Sophie. Then he put me out of my misery, "and before you ask, yes I know about you and Sophie." Could he read my mind? "And it's not just me who does; absolutely everyone has picked up on it."

"I don't know what you're talking about," I said defiantly, even though I could tell that there was literally no chance of him believing me. "So who are all of these so-called people who supposedly think that I'm allegedly seeing her?" I was babbling to the extent that if he hadn't already cracked the world's easiest riddle then I'm sure that my horrendous lying would have given me away.

"Nobody thinks it," he began, "everybody knows it. I'm not a detective, but please consider the following evidence. Exhibit A, I've seen her coming out of your office lots of times, she locks the door when she goes in, you only ever seem to relax when she's just left and it's fair to say that she has a long standing reputation for that sort of thing. So how does the defendant plead?"

I could feel my face starting to boil up. My thoughts were now focused on Janice. Did she know? If she did then she would almost certainly have had me castrated for crimes against womanhood.

Fortunately his psychic powers (or my predictability) knew no bounds. "Before you ask, Janice hasn't picked up on it yet, or at least if she has then she hasn't mentioned it to me. But I don't see how she could have missed it and for all I know she might be the only one."

I was desperate to cling on to my lie. "Well none of those supposed rumours have even the slightest hint of truth behind them." I avoided making any eye contact, "There is nothing going on with Sophie and me, so Janice has literally nothing whatsoever to worry about. Anyway if she doesn't like her then that's her problem. I don't even know why she hates her so much anyway."

He smirked, "you're rambling. And as for your question, it's dead easy, why do any women hate each other? It's all to do with jealousy. Think about it, Sophie's younger than Janice, she's better looking than her and she's already had more promotions in a much shorter period of time. Do you remember when Janice used to appear in all of the trade magazines? 'The new hope for the City' that's what they used to call her. Now none of them care about her because she doesn't look like Sophie. The sad truth is that short of a miracle the only way Janice will ever get another promotion is if she manages to find a photo of Colin having sex with a goat." We both chuckled at the futility of gender relations in the City, and then he looked me directly in the eyes. "Look mate, I know what's been going on. I'm not stupid."

"Ok, fine," I said. "There's no point denying it anymore, I have been seeing her." My big dramatic revelation was met by him contemptuously rolling his eyes. "But it's over now and we haven't done anything since I met Venus."

"Wow!" he responded with mock shock, "that means that you must have gone a whole eight days. Oh my god Floyd, that's really loyal of you, how have you managed to cope?" He shook his head dismissively and then shouted to a group of old punks across the bar, "Hey guys, you should meet my friend Floyd, he's gone a whole eight days without seeing his mistress. Do you reckon that he's earned some kind of medal?" His shouting was met with indifference, but it still gave him the right to act smug. He turned back and took a long gulp from his pint, then he dried his mouth with his forearm and dragged our conversation into the gutter, "so is she any good?" he asked.

I was taken a-back; if this was a comedy film then this is the point when I would have spat out my beer. "What did you say?" I asked with a mixture of shock and disdain.

"You heard me. Is she any good?"

"Is who any good at what?"

"I mean Sophie of course, is she good at it?"

"What the hell has that got to do with anything?"

"I'm trying to figure out why you would want to jeopardise the very enviable thing that you have with her by going for this other girl. I mean let's be honest, she has a silly pixie-like name and it's not like you're going to marry her is it?"

"Well no," I said, "but that's not the point. Besides, I like her name, and I do actually like her."

He tried not to giggle, "Ok, so what's she got that Sophie doesn't?"

"Lots of things," I answered defensively.

"Such as what? Give me something to work with, what's special about her? What's she got?"

"Well she has a personality for a start."

He scoffed, "personalities are overrated at this age." I wondered if he knew how much of an arse it made him sound when he said things like that. "Besides, you're clearly not over Penelope, if you were then you wouldn't have gone anywhere near Sophie." He took another drink, "Don't get me wrong, I know her type. She's the sort of girl you can have a good time with. She's a nice girl and she's easygoing, but you wouldn't take her to meet your mother would you?" I shook my head, "and before I have to get sugar lumps for your high horse it's important to say that there's nothing wrong with girls like her. In fact some of the best times I've ever had have been spent with girls like her. They're great, it doesn't have to mean anything much to you, it doesn't have to mean much to them, and if you're both on the same page then it's wonderful."

"I don't know about that," I said, "I don't ever feel like I'm getting anything out of it when I spend time with her. At first it felt like a thrill, but now it just feels kind of cheap."

He leaned forward with all of the impatience of a grouchy old college lecturer. "Jesus Floyd, do you ever listen to yourself? As far as I know no-one has ever held a gun to your head and forced you to do it." He sighed, "What is your big obsession with trying to fall in love anyway? One in three marriages end in divorce and most of the ones that don't are unhappy from the start." He took a short sip from his pint, "I've known a lot of married women and none of them are in love. Some of my best friends are married and lots of them feel trapped, they're trapped in well-meaning ruts because someone like you told them that it was a good idea to settle down at 25."

"Have you ever been in love?" I asked him in an attempt to cut through the bravado and see the real him.

He raised his eyebrows. "It's hard to say, I once thought that I was. That was a long time ago, and it wasn't real love. It was just bullshit. It began with things like dates and dinners and long walks in the park, but it was boring. It didn't last long because a few things were said and then everything got a bit ugly. I walked out of it and then she went off with someone else."

For a few seconds the mood changed. He looked down at his feet and started stirring his beer with his finger. After years of knowing him this was one of the first times that I had ever seen him lose his swagger. He didn't like being in the spotlight, he bit down on his bottom lip to the point that it looked like drawing blood.

"I'm sorry" I said, almost apologetically. I wanted to ask him more about this girl. I wanted to know what had happened and what she had done to him, and I wanted to know if it was that breakup that was responsible for the marks on his arms. I wanted to ask him about all of this, but I was too afraid. I don't know what I was afraid of, but something stopped me from really seizing the opportunity to get to know my friend.

He rolled his eyes and slowly shook his head. "It taught me a lot of things. It taught me that chasing girls isn't worth the effort. It taught me that making love is usually just something that deluded people think that they're doing while someone else is fucking them. If our generation has a crowning achievement it's that we killed it. If real love ever existed then it's all but gone, it's been sold down the river and it's been replaced by commercialised bullshit and tacky gifts that disguise themselves as love. We're a generation that really needs it though, have you noticed that every expectant young mother to be always says the same thing? They all say that they want a baby because they want somebody who can love them unconditionally. Those aren't the words of selfless parents, those are the words of a desperately lost and love deprived generation. The problem is that they're too late, we're all too late."

"And you don't even want to try to find anything deeper than that?" I asked. "You don't aspire to raise yourself up beyond the levels of cynicism?"

"No I don't. Not right now anyway. I don't want anyone to be able to do that to me ever again. I'm not in the City because I love finance. I'm in the City because it's a means to an end and I want to use it. I don't want to be an economist all my life. I want to be an idol. I want to be able to look at the television screen and see me staring back at me. I want to know that every school boy in the country wants to grow up to be me and that every girl in the world wants to grow up to be with me. When I'm old and immobile I don't want to wish that I had spent my time better. When I'm 40 I'll probably settle down with some dead eyed girl who only wants me for what she thinks she can get out of me. It's ok, I won't have any illusions. I know that we won't love each other but we'll probably stay together through a mixture of convenience and resentment that we've learnt to hide behind fraudulent smiles. It's not anything that I'm looking forward to, and until it happens I don't even want to think about all of that stuff."

"Why not?"

"I don't want to because it's so depressing. We come from the most materialistic generation there has ever been and also the least happy. We're the first generation who can do all of our shopping from a desk and yet we pop anti depressants as if they were Tic-Tacs. If we hate who are then it's no problem because we're the first generation who can go to a doctor and have them erase our whole identities and let us start all over again as someone else. None of that will change, it will only get worse. Once you accept that this is the reality then you accept that there's no need for any of that so-called chivalrous stuff. If you do all of that romantic stuff for a woman but you can't get her a big fat ring then you're as good as dead to her."

"So where does Brogan fit into all of this?"

"She doesn't" he said very firmly, "we're just friends."

"Do you honestly expect me to believe that?"

"It's the truth" he said. "We talk and we hang out online, but nothing else has ever happened."

"In that case why do you talk to her?"

"Because she's cool" he said. "And because she's nothing like all of the women at work. In fact I doubt that she even knows what FTSE 100 means. She's open, she's honest and she's nice, isn't that enough? Does it really need to be anything more than that?" We could have carried on talking about it but neither of us really wanted to have a full-blown argument. "Anyway", he said, "it's not my time on the couch yet, and we're here to talk about you." I sat back, waiting for his verbal slings and arrows. "The problem you've got is nothing to do with Brogan. The problem is that you've messed with Sophie's emotions and now you want to cover yourself. Can I ask you a question?"

I nodded.

"I bet that you built up to sex when you were first with Penelope and I bet that you waited and waited until you really got to know her first, didn't you?" I nodded, "and the reason for that was obvious, it was because you were nervous and you wanted her to know that you were a decent guy in case you weren't very good at it, am I right?" I nodded again. "Whereas now that you're out of that rut, and now that you know how to do it properly you've become like the rest of us mere mortals and sex has become your ice breaker and your oh so great personality has become a secondary concern." He went in for the proverbial kill. "In short, what I'm saying is that you went for Sophie because she was there. She was willing, she was easy and it was a damn site more fun than getting to know her."

"It wasn't like that," I said. "Besides, there are about one million reasons why I could never have a proper relationship with Sophie."

"That's only because in your silly frantic head you've already defined your relationship as a purely sexual one. Listen I know what she's like and I know that she has a reputation, but at the moment you're the only guy she's seeing."

"So what are you saying?"

"I'm saying that she likes you. And she'll be upset if you break up with her."

"But it's not like we go on proper full-on dates or anything, so it's not like it's a real relationship."

"Not in the same way as you and Penelope were in a so called 'real relationship', but she might not see it that way." He leaned in a bit closer, as if to stress that he was actually being serious. "She can't call you her boyfriend because she's your boss, but remember that one of the other guys that she's close to is Colin, and if you upset her then she'll almost certainly ask him to fire you." BOOM! "The other point is that there's no such thing as a proper relationship. Every relationship is different. What do you think about those weird couples that you see on the internet? Are you saying that they can't have relationships?"

"No, but that's not really the point is it?"

"Sure it is, and what about gay people? They're different from you, well maybe not too different" he winked, "but does that mean that they can't have proper relationships? The point is that what's not a relationship to you might be to her, even if you think that you're just messing around then it could mean a lot more to her." He did a dismissive waving gesture that suggested everything he had just said was irrelevant to his main point. "Anyway, the nub of the issue comes down to one simple question. Are you utterly 100% sure that it doesn't mean anything more to her?"

"Yes"

"Has she explicitly said that?"

"No. Not in those words."

"Have you explicitly asked her?"

"No."

"So for all you know she could see it totally differently from you. What you also have to bear in mind is that you are always banging on about what a crisis you're in and all of that nonsense about not being able to think straight. With that in mind you're not necessarily the best judge of your own actions are you?"

"So what do you think I should do?"

"It's simple. Don't let anything happen with Venus. Just drop her and pretend that nothing ever happened."

I almost spat out my drink. "But I want something to happen with her. I like her."

"You asked for my advice mate. "Listen, I might act like an idiot and I might call you a fag from time to time, but you know that beneath all of that I'm your friend. I don't like these gay emotional chats either but I'm trying to help. Whether you like it or not you have to stop seeing one of them and at the end of the day Venus isn't in a position to fire you. What you have to remember is that if Sophie gets Colin to fire you then you'll be unemployed during a recession."

"So you think that I should leave Venus? Do you think that I should also end things with Sophie?"

"No, that's the worst thing you could do. She's got you in the same position that Colin had her. We both know that Colin only stopped seeing her because he was bored of her, well it's like that only she's him and you're her. You have no choice but to keep going until she gets bored of you."

"That's not likely to happen any time soon," I said. "She's already sent me two texts today. To be honest if I hadn't spent yesterday with Venus then I would probably have gone to see her this afternoon."

"So you see her outside of working hours and you go round to her house?" He shook his head, "mate, you're fucked." Then he smiled at his unintended pun.

Chapter 15

Sophie's office overlooked St Paul's Cathedral, and her picturesque view was made all the more spectacular by the fact that she was 25 stories off the ground. Her office was much bigger than mine, much tidier than mine and had far more visitors than mine. She had only been in there for a few months but she had already given it her own touch and turned it into one of the most intimidating rooms in the building.

She wore her power well, she had to. She walked with a strut, she projected confidence, and she made us believe that she was comfortable in the knowledge that she could either make or break any of our careers any time she wanted. The truth is that she wasn't; the fragile side of her that I had seen in the pub was the part of her that no-one else could ever see. She had no choice; the board was so bloodthirsty that if they ever sensed any weakness then she would be finished. She was very convincing though, and that meant that all of the trade unions feared her and all of the graduates and the new starts were desperate to impress her. Her ascent up the company had been unparalleled; when I had started she was an office skivvy, but somewhere along the line I had become comfortable in my apathy, in contrast she put in the extra hours and the hard work and now she was my boss.

She hadn't been in a great mood recently. From what I had heard she had spent her last few days locked away in her office with a set of big daunting spreadsheets, a bunch of contracts and a red pen. Apparently Colin was demanding more cuts and had given her the impossible task of reducing the running costs of the company by 10%, so in essence her job was now to fire people. This isn't as easy as it sounds, it can be really complicated getting rid of people; most of us don't get paid enough to warrant sacking, and the few people who do are the untouchable ones who are demanding the cuts in the first place.

***

It hadn't been a great day; the only slight highlight had been a short chat with Venus on Facebook and a 10 minute cigarette break that I had taken with George. We had talked about the upcoming election, he was going to vote Labour and I was probably going to abstain altogether. The point that he made is that most people weren't hugely affected by which party was in office because they all do the same things, but people in his position were because if the Tories got in then they would probably make it easier to sack minimum wage workers and cut unemployment benefit. He sounded almost proud as he loyally told me that it was the Labour party that he had to thank for the few rights that he had, although I couldn't share his sycophancy for the same party that had brought us into endless wars and given us a recession. In his defence I guess it's easier to be a political puritan when you've got a car, a degree, a comfortable income and a bunch of first-world problems.

"I can't say I'm too excited about any of the parties, they're all the same" I said. "None of them give a shit about anything other than feathering their own nests and winning over people like Colin. Don't you remember what happened last time? What do you think will happen differently if they win this time?"

"Not a lot" he replied, "but they won't make as many cuts and they won't let poor people starve to death." I raised my eyebrows, I was somewhat surprised that his expectations for our government was so low that it amounted to whether or not they were willing to let people starve to death. I don't know which of us was more cynical of the political class; on one hand he had lower expectations than I did, but on the other he bothered to vote and try to engage with process while I didn't even do that.

As I looked at George I tried to put myself in his shoes, but it was impossible. He worked for minimum wage and he had nothing to fall back on if it all went wrong. I thought about how bad it would feel to know that you were doomed to cleaning up other people's stuff and your only break would come from retirement 40 years later. I thought about how I had turned away from him in Trafalgar Square and how he would never have done that to me. As I stubbed out my cigarette I thought again about whether or not he had noticed me.

***

By the time that I arrived at her office most of my Venus inspired optimism had been replaced by an unusual and unpleasant emotional equilibrium that lay somewhere between shaking with nerves and being frozen in fear. I knocked on her door before I walked in. There were books everywhere and she was wearing her hair up, so there was an inappropriately formal tone to the backdrop. "Just a minute" she called out before she looked up to see who I was.

She was visibly stressed; all of the big purple veins in her forehead were threatening to burst at any moment as she rubbed her big tired eyes. After a few seconds she turned to face me, the whirring noise from her computer was the only thing breaking our silence. She rested her chin in her hands and forced herself to wear a pained smile and pointed her eyes towards the empty seat. I sat down and tried to smile back at her, "has it been a tough day?" I asked sympathetically.

"You could say that," she said as she sipped from a glass of water. "The figures this month aren't showing any real signs of improvements. It's been really tough and our key shareholders are getting cold feet, and can you blame them? Needless to say it's become an absolute nightmare trying to get anything done."

"I didn't know that things are so bad" I said sympathetically.

She nodded as she leaned back in her seat and looked at me wistfully. "It's worse than we thought. There about one million different pressures kicking our asses and it feels like anything that we can do can only make it worse. It's not like the recession is going to end any time soon is it?" She sighed, and then she stood up and poured two glasses of red wine from a bottle she took out from below her desk. She passed one across the table to me and walked over to the window with hers.

It was the first time since the pub in Shoreditch that I had heard her talking seriously or seen her showing any trace of weakness. She may have been trying to hide her stress below a layer of makeup and front but I could see through it and she looked fragile and scared. She turned her back to me as she sipped her wine and looked out across the city. Some other lights were dotted around the Square Mile, but the main skyline was dark, although we could hear the commotion and sirens from the streets below as clearly as we would have from the ground floor.

"We're friends aren't we?" she asked coldly and blankly after a pregnant pause. I nodded; she could see my reflection in the glass so she didn't bother to turn round. She rubbed her eyes again, "So if we're friends then please can you do the friendly thing and get me out of here, I've been in here all day and I'm losing the will to stay any longer. Why don't we go out and get dinner or a drink? We can even catch a movie or something."

"We can't," I said. "I would love to do all of those things but there's something that I think we need to talk to you about first."

"Floyd, Is everything ok?"

I took a short slurp of my wine, "It's just that I don't know how you're going to take this" I said quietly. She heard the apprehension in my voice and turned around.

"Is there something wrong?" she sounded concerned.

"Yes, It's just that," I forced a cough so that I could have an extra couple of seconds to think about how I was going to word this, "it's just that at the moment things are starting to get really busy right now. They're really busy for both of us..."

"I know," she interrupted, "and I know how I must sound sometimes and I'm sorry about that. You have absolutely no idea how grateful I am every time that you let me vent to you like this."

"It's just that", I forced another cough, "It's just that with everything that's going on and everything that is about to happen I just don't think I can be there for you in quite the same way as I have been. Do you understand? It's just that because of all of everything that's going on I don't really think that we should see each other anymore."

"Not see each other? How would thank work? I know that things are busy but we both work in the same building so what are you talking about?"

"Precisely, we work in the same building and I mean on top of that you're also my boss," I said in an attempt to feed her a work/ protocol related narrative to make it easier. "It's just that you know what this place is like, word gets around very quickly and some people are already starting to talk," she nodded. I couldn't tell if she understood me or not, it wasn't as if I was speaking cryptically, I could hardly have been any more obvious. "The thing is that I like you a lot and I think you're a nice girl, but because of what people are saying it might be worth us thinking about taking a step back. I just think that maybe we shouldn't really be spending so much time together, what do you think?"

After a few seconds of silence she took her eyes off me and looked out the window again. "That's ok" she said. "If that's what you wanted to talk to me about then it's alright, I understand." She turned to face the window again and took another drink. "I like you too Floyd, and it's been fun, but maybe you're right." She rubbed her eyes again and took a long gulp of wine. "Thank you for coming to see me, but you should go now because I've got far too much work to do."

"Are you sure?"

"Yeah, I'm totally sure."

***

I couldn't get her out of my head that night. What if I had really upset her? She was clearly stressed already, had I just made everything even worse? I went onto Facebook to look for clues, but she was offline and she hadn't updated her page or left any new comments for over a week.

The next day I went out of my way to avoid her, which wasn't very hard because she was obviously avoiding me too. I sat in my office chatting to Venus online when an irritable Steven came in. He hadn't bothered to knock and had just walked right over to my desk. "You're total fucking moron. I take it that you broke up with her."

"Yeah," I responded, "and please don't use that as an opening line in conversation ever again. I did it last night, why?"

"Because everyone is saying that she's been acting like an absolute bitch all day. The unions are especially angry and are talking about strikes and that sort of thing. The rumour that they're spreading is that she's just announced that she's getting rid of about half of the janitors and cleaning staff."

I was stunned; and I could only draw the ridiculously depressing conclusion that my inability to say no had just got a load of low skilled workers fired. All that I could think about was George, it wasn't as if he had done anything wrong, and he had no skills so it wasn't as if he could simply walk into a well paid job somewhere else. I didn't want Steven to know about the minor crisis that was playing out in my head, so I tried to look like I was exceptionally calm about everything. "Oh right" I said with a stiff British hesitation in my voice, "but is it true or is it all just innuendo?"

"The jury's out on that one. The unions are probably just sabre rattling. I'm not going to lie though, there's a large part of me that thinks good for her. It's about time that we got rid of some of those shit munchers, most of them are ass holes anyway." He sat on the chair opposite me, "but it won't end with the shit munchers will it? They're just the start, this is like a chess game for them, and the atmosphere around here is so absolutely cancerous that almost any one of us could be in the firing line."

"No we won't" I said with a sigh, "people like us are cost neutral. We bring in just as much money as we take. I don't bring any new business but I don't lose any and I'm needed to service the people that I work with, so are you. I've given it some thought and it really doesn't make any financial sense for them to have a cull."

"Yes it does, shareholders love downsizing. It'll show all of the so called experts that they're serious about efficiency and cutting costs. In their minds it'll look absolutely brilliant. It'll be a case of saying goodbye to excess wasters and hello to improved market confidence and good write-ups in the Investors Chronicle and the FT. This is not the time for being a maverick; it's the time for keeping your head low. The problem is that in your stupidity you've given her the perfect excuse to make sure that you're one of the unlucky ones. Mate, as I've said before I like you, but you're asking for trouble, and it's for that reason that I think you've done something totally and utterly fucking stupid."

"I know you do," I snapped, "but I've done it now. At least I can stop looking over my shoulder and get on with my life. I can concentrate on me for a while and I have the chance to see where things might go with Venus without having to worry about what'll happen if she finds out about Sophie."

"Well?" he said, "What will happen when she finds out about Sophie?"

"Nothing, it's over so there's nothing for her to find out."

"So you think that she'll be happy to know that only a couple of days after your first date you were thinking about the best way to break up with your boss? Don't be so stupid."

"It's not like that." I said. "And anyway when it comes to this sort of thing you definitely don't have any right to judge me. Do I have to remind you that you're the one who's in an electronic relationship with a teenager?"

The atmosphere had become far too tense and we both knew it. Neither of us wanted a fight so he didn't retaliate, instead he turned to leave. When he was at the door he tried to save the mood and make me feel extremely guilty in the process. "Floyd, despite what we may both say, we are friends. I know how it feels when you get caught up in a woman, and whether you choose to believe it or not I am actually looking out for you."

"I know," I said, "thanks."

As he quietly left the room I pulled a bottle of wine out from my drawer and poured a small glass. I looked up at my clock and tried to wish away the next eight hours or so while I took a drink. I managed to relax a bit when I saw George. As far as he knew he was safe, which made me feel a bit less shitty about everything that was going on. He had done the sensible thing and joined one of the trade unions because it was much harder to sack them, which is why we both thought that he was in the clear.

***

Later that night I had a frantic phone call from my parents. My father was choking back his tears as he told me that there was bad news. My grandmother's health had deteriorated further and she had taken another turn for the worse. She was very old and we had been expecting it for a while, but it was still a shock, and with that in mind I packed a bag and went home for the weekend.

Chapter 16

No-one in my family was surprised when she died, but that didn't make it any easier. We loved her but the truth was that we had been expecting it for a long time; she was 92 and she had been getting progressively weaker for a long time. She had once been a proud and intellectual woman, but towards the end she had become frail, fragile and forgetful. I missed the grandmother who I had grown up with, and I desperately empathised with the one I was losing.

If her physical condition was deteriorating then her accommodation didn't help. It was a well meaning but underfunded little place, and despite the best intentions of everyone involved it couldn't help but fall short. If she had fallen ill before the crash then it would have been different because we could have put her somewhere nicer, but the sad truth was that she wasn't well enough to live alone, and because my parents had either wasted or lost all of their money they couldn't afford anywhere better.

***

As we walked in she looked so small and tired. Despite her surroundings she was smiling, and she had enough kindness in her eyes to remind me of why I loved her so much. Speaking to her had always a wonderful and stimulating experience that was like delving into the most brilliant history book about London. In her 92 years she had seen so much change, she had lived through so much; she had seen the rise and fall of fascism, she had seen the Berlin Wall being put up and then taken down, she had lived through the birth of television, she had been out on the streets mourning the day that Churchill died and she had stayed up late watching as man landed on the moon. She had seen it all from London, she had lived there all her life and had seen it transform into a completely new city. The ship yards were gone, the factories were gone and the smoke had cleared up, since then the airports had arrived, different communities had emerged, shopping centres had been built and multinational capitalism had come to dominate the skyline and the economy.

She hadn't taken all of the changes lying down, like my father she was a real political animal, albeit she batted for the other side. She had spent her life as a trade unionist and a convicted socialist. She was a product of the times; she had worked through austerity, she had lead local strikes and she had spent a decade as a Labour Party councillor. I wondered what she had been like when she was my age; has she been happy? What had she dreamt of? So many post-war dreams had turned to dust and become nothing more than urban fantasies. She had lived a wonderful life and she had so much to be proud of, but the tragic part was that as she entered her last days she couldn't remember any of it.

We all hugged her and sat down in a semi circle around her bed, and then she sat up and smiled through her discomfort. It was a smile of warmth but it wasn't a smile of familiarity. She looked pleasantly surprised to see us, but she also looked like she was trying to remember who we were. My mother reached out and took her hand, and then she smiled as if to reassure her that we were family. I watched the closeness and affection in her manner and wished that I knew her well enough to act in kind.

I felt a guilty chill as I thought about how rarely I had visited. This was the first time that I had seen her in months and there wasn't any excuse for it. There had been a time when I had sent regular letters and made regular phone calls, but somewhere along the line they had dried up. My father was overcome with emotions. He had always been worried about this day and now he was confronted by it and he didn't know what to do. I didn't know how to respond either, I was desperate not to cry though, and I forced myself not to. It's not that I didn't want to, but I felt like I had to try and be as strong as possible at a time when my parents couldn't be. There were tears forming in his eyes, but I remained steadfast. I may have looked hollow but my forced and controlled demeanour was more of a mask than a feeling, and I was using it to guard myself from my emotions. My mother took him outside with one of the nurses and left me alone with her.

I moved forward on my chair to get closer to her. I didn't know what to say, so I smiled and took out the photo album and showed her some pictures of us together. At first she looked a bit overwhelmed but a small happy glimmer of what looked like recognition formed in her eyes as she scanned an old photo of me, Penelope and her sitting together below a big green tree in the back garden of her home. The photo had been taken on a beautiful summer afternoon during one of my last visits. As she scanned the album I held her hand and drew a pattern on her palm with my thumb while I remembered the weekly visits we had made when I was growing up. At the time they had felt insignificant, but if I could have gone back to do them again then I would have done it in a heartbeat.

We spoke for a while longer, although it was me that did most of the talking. I told her all about what I was doing, I don't know how much of it made any sense to her but she was clearly happy to hear my voice. When my parents came back I was still holding her hand, I didn't want to let her go. There was an uncomfortable apologetic knot in my stomach. I knew that this was going to be the last time I ever saw her. I knew that there was a good chance she had already forgotten who I was, and I knew that even if she remembered it now then it was unlikely that she would die knowing that she had a grandson.

***

I was having lunch with Janice when I found out. As soon as I saw the call coming through from my father I knew what he was going to say before he said it. It was an almost business-like conversation; it was devoid of any of the raw emotion from our visit because formalising it made it all seem a bit less real. I told him that I would be there for him and that I would help him with the funeral arrangements, but I said it in the same manner I would use to reassure a client, I even finished by telling him that he should call me if he 'needed anything'.

The fact that she was 92 hadn't made it any easier for him; losing your mother is still losing your mother. They had still been very close. In contrast my life has been shaped as much by electronics and the media as it has been by my parents. As soon as I was old enough to appreciate moving pictures and pre- recorded sounds I stopped seeing them as the gods in my life. Generation Debt has to be both the most connected and the most isolated generation in history. Cable TV, mobile phones and the internet have all conspired to ensure that we're never alone for too long, but they've also ensured that the majority of our interaction is superficial at best.

It was a long time ago that close-knit family games-nights were replaced by evenings spent around the television, but it was only a few years ago that they were replaced by people locking themselves in their bedrooms with laptops. We've been left in a permanent state of virtual contact and the kind of tokenistic friendships that bloom online. Being alone was hard for me, having spent years living with Penelope, I had become so dependent on other people that I had forgotten how to spend time by myself.

I was as surprised by own detached tone as I was by the fact that she was gone. I felt too distant and cold, I didn't like that we were discussing her like she was an abstract piece of stock. I sighed at my own insensitivity and asked Janice when she had last seen her parents.

"I saw my mum a few weeks ago actually. She was in town to catch up with friends, so she came round for a cup of tea and a chat."

"How was it?" I asked as I lit a comforting cigarette.

"It was really awkward. The whole thing felt so staged. I brought out my only china and got fancy biscuits and everything. But that made it worse because it all felt even more unnatural and forced. It felt like neither of us wanted to be there and there was so much mutual bitterness and apathy that we were papering over for the sake of keeping up appearances, which only made it more obvious that it was there. We didn't have to act like that. There were only the two of us so no-one would ever have known. It was obvious that we were both only doing it out of some kind of misplaced sense of obligation towards something. On the plus side I'm fairly sure that she found it just as horrible as I did."

I smiled and shook my head. "It sounds pretty awful. In fact I would go as far as saying that you make me glad for my family. Was it always so bad? Can you remember when it went sour? When did you first realise that you had become so removed from her?"

She thought about it for a few seconds, "I don't know, as far back as I can remember we've been virtual strangers. I genuinely can't remember ever feeling any warmth towards her. I know that sounds horrible but it's true. What you have to understand is that when I was growing up she wouldn't let me out of her sight, so I was around her all the time. When I was a teenager she was so controlling and demanding that she made everything into a battle. Even when I became an adult nothing I could ever do was good enough, after 20 years of it I finally lost all interest in trying to form a bond with her and even stopped sending cards on Mother's Day. I don't like the fact that I act like that, I don't like the person who I become when I'm talking about her."

"I know how you feel", I said. "I always feel a burning sense of guilt when I get annoyed with my parents, although they're nowhere near as bad as that. We don't fight or anything, but I couldn't tell you any of their favourite books, films or musicians. I don't even know what they do in their spare time. The part I find hard is that these aren't secrets, they're the sorts of things that I even know about the janitors at our work, and yet I don't know anything about my own parents, how strange is that?"

She nodded slowly in agreement and reached out across the table to hold my hand. I took a long draw from my cigarette while the loneliness of what I had just said sank in.

***

Now that I thought things were officially 'over' with Sophie I had decided in my still frantic mind that it was the time to take my next big step with Venus. The problem was that although everything was going well I knew that there were some things that weren't right. We could waste away hours talking about nothing in particular, but she was so much better than me that I also knew that I couldn't imagine myself being prepared to really talk to her in depth and really feeling like I could share who I was with her. I was intimidated by the fact that she didn't seem to have any insecurities, her self-confidence and her perfect looks gave her an armour that I didn't want to penetrate in case she learnt how much more perfect she was. I was scared of letting her know who I was in case she didn't like me anymore. I know that honesty needs to be the foundation of a good relationship and although it had only been a few weeks I already felt like I was keeping too many secrets.

I never felt at home around any of her friends, they were all bourgeoisie, pretentious and proud, and they all had stupid nicknames (Pop, Bang and Shhh). They all worked in world-saving do-gooder jobs and I found it hard to relate to their collective brand of sanctimonious bullshit. They whined and moaned about the most inane and banal things; independent cinema, the question of whether or not the Labour Party had sold out their founding principles and the high price of organic food. I only met them a couple of time but I could tell that the feeling was mutual. They didn't seem impressed by me and I could feel them judging me as soon as I told them where I worked.

In fairness it wasn't as if Janice had tried any harder with Venus. The one time she met her she was pretty non-committal and indifferent. It was a really frustrating coffee because I could see poor Venus desperately trying to ignite conversation by asking lots of questions while Janice let her flounder. When Venus went to the toilet I leaned in to ask her why she was being so anti-social. "Because I don't think there's enough to her" she said calmly. "No offence, I mean she's nice enough, and I can see why you like her, but she's so up herself that she's almost a bit of a caricature. She has a naive and childish worldview and, again without wishing to upset you, she's got rebound written all over her." Before I could say anything in her defence she returned to the now very frosty table.

To his credit Steven tried his best. I wanted her to meet him because she had heard about him through the grapevine and she had kept asking me if he was anywhere near as bad as everyone else kept making out. I kept saying he wasn't, so when we went for a glass of wine with him I was terrified about what he would say and do. I had asked him to be on his best and most socially acceptable behaviour, which felt like a payback for the numerous times I had sat in silence while he chatted up women and disgraced himself. This time he was at his charming best, he laid on the complements thick and fast and didn't even make one single gay joke about me. Apparently when I went to the bar he told her about how brilliant he thought I was, all things considered it was a masterful performance in friendship and deception.

Despite my reservations I was feeling stressed and desperate to get away for a while, so I asked her if she wanted to escape somewhere for the weekend after the funeral was over. We had only been together for a few weeks, but in my quarter life crisis frame of mind this was long enough for us to be thinking about these things. It was rather like when I asked her out, because I felt safe in the knowledge that she would probably say no, so I was actually quite alarmed when she agreed. Venus was smarter, better looking and more confident than me. This meant that when she had said it was a good idea I was actually very nervous. Why was she agreeing to do so much so quickly? Surely she could do better than me? In time her superiority would be confirmed, that weekend would be the last time I saw her.

Chapter 17

The funeral was only the second one that I had ever been to; the first had been for an uncle who had died from a heart attack when I was nine. I can remember feeling sad and confused, but I was too young to fully comprehend what it all meant. My parents had never given me the 'death' talk when I was young, so almost all that I knew about human mortality came from television and books. I had grown up with a tidal wave of pictures of celebrity births and iconic funerals, all of which had given me a somewhat plastic and glamorised vision of life and death. All of this was punctured when I was 14 and a girl called Sandra from my physics class was killed by her father. We held a two minute silence at school the next day and the teacher said we could share any memories we had of her, but the problem was that there were 30 of us in the class and not one of us had been her friend. The investigation uncovered that he had regularly beaten and abused her since she was a child. We were all shocked because she had always been so gentle and quiet, but that just meant that she had suffered in silence. I followed the story to its sorry conclusion, which saw him being locked up for 30 years, but that made it seem like even more of a waste. I hadn't gone to her funeral, none of us had, but she was on my mind that day..

Getting dressed for a funeral is such an unusual feeling as it's the one time that have to put on your best suit in order to not get noticed. If it had been another context I would have looked $1 million, but on that day I was only doing it to fit in. I debated whether or not to put on aftershave, somehow it felt inappropriate so I decided not to.

As we walked into the church hall we heard the strains of Piano Sonata 2 in B Flat Minor, which is a tune I will never be able to listen to again without thinking of her. The service felt so detached, it was a big, grand, old fashioned church hall but the priest didn't live up to his setting. He sounded as mournful as he could but it still felt like he was basically going through the motions and talking without any real feeling, I'm not sure if he had ever met her before. The running order had only been worked out at the last moment. She hadn't been religious, but my father in particular was adamant that she had been moving in that direction during her last days and I had no desire to argue with him about how he wanted to bury his mother.

The bible readings were nice and comfortingly agnostic, but I had a real sense of admiration for him as he read a eulogy for her. He spoke about growing up with a strong visionary woman and highlighted her numerous concrete achievements and the hurdles that she had overcome to be there. His voice wobbled as he recounted his happy childhood, I could feel his regret when he talked earnestly and openly about the times he hadn't lived up to her high expectations. "Every time I let her down it only made me want to please her more, she was such a spirit and such an inspiration that I couldn't be contented with her love unless I knew that I also had her respect. There were times when I wasn't worthy of it, but she was always there for me and she always forgave me. I always felt guilty because I have never had to forgive her for anything, and her capacity to love has always been limitless." A tear ran down his face, "And you have no idea how much I wish that I could have had even one more day with her." His speech was punctuated by the cracking of thunder through the thin roof. It felt like the Gods were punishing her counterfeit Christianity by giving us some of the worst weather we had seen for months.

A small group of wet mourners had come from across London; some of them were former friends and colleagues from her days with the council, and some of them were nurses from the home. Of course most of her friends, and the majority of the people who she had shared her life with, were already gone. One of the tragedies of the funeral was just how few people she had left.

It was a slow muddy trudge from the church to the cemetery. There was a really nice moment when I looked behind me and saw the line of people behind me, there weren't many of them but it was nice to know that she would be missed. The weather meant that we couldn't savour her last moments above ground and we couldn't remember them in quite the way that we wanted to. The priest, who was hiding below an umbrella, began to hurry through her last rites. Despite the rain everyone around me was in tears, I was trying to stay strong and refrain from crying, but it wasn't working. The sight of my mother's tears was enough to make me give in. I could feel my eyes burning up, and then I felt Janice put her arm around me and held my hand. I was grateful for her warmth as I sank my head into her shoulder and let my tears run down my cheeks. It was hard to believe that all that remained of this once loving woman was a wooden casket with lifeless limbs inside it. I kept my head low and mumbled a few loose prayers in the unlikely hope that someone was listening. At that point there is nothing that I wouldn't have given to be able to believe in something.

***

Afterwards I asked Janice to keep an eye on things while I took a quiet walk around the cemetery. In the sun it would have been a beautiful and peaceful place, but from below my umbrella it felt gloomy and punishing. I had always been relatively sheltered from death, but that didn't stop me from thinking about the thousands of lives that were buried below me.

I studied the old tombstones, so many of them had died so young. I couldn't help but feel an emotional swelling in my throat as I walked over the bodies of people who had died as mere children. They were particularly tragic, they were so innocent and uncorrupted and now they were no more than a distant memory and name on a stone. The children had never had the chance to make their mark on the world, there was no one around anymore who could even remember them or talk fondly of them, they had neither futures nor legacies. When I returned to her grave I wanted to cry again. I found a quiet bench below some mossy covering. I smoked a cigarette and watched from afar as another body was lowered into the ground.

***

Janice came back to my house afterwards for a coffee. I was quite touched to see that I had got a card in the mail from Steven. It was a 'thinking of you' card that was free of swagger and obnoxiousness. *"Dear Floyd, I hope you're as well as you can be. I remember when I lost my granddad two years ago, it made me regret all of the letters I had never written, but it made me very grateful for every time I ever spent with him. If you ever want to talk then I'm there for you. Steven."* It was a lot like the card I had sent him when his favourite aunt was in hospital, both had been caring cards but I doubted that either of us would ever explicitly mention them again. One of the tragedies of my relationship with him is that we have to write stuff like that. The sad part is that if it weren't for his male bravado and my neuroticism then we could say that sort of thing and not be afraid of what the other would think if we showed our vulnerabilities.

The house was in a mess because I hadn't properly cleaned it for a few weeks. We climbed over piles of my stuff and went through to the kitchen. I only had instant stuff so the coffee was pretty weak and watery. At first we talked about work, she had started to apply for new jobs all across the country. After badmouthing our bosses she told me about the drink she had the night before with her friend April. April was an old school friend of hers who had been living in a metropolitan and politically correct fairytale until she had found out that her husband was cheating on her. Now she had left him and she was running a successful fair-trade clothing company and had asked Janice what she thought about working together. At first she was against it, she didn't want to risk ruining their friendship in the way so many business partners do, but now she was giving it a bit more thought.

We also talked about Steven, after everything that had happened I wanted to escape from my own thoughts and find out more about his internet relationship. Janice stressed that it was strictly plutonic, but I didn't believe her. How could Steven, a man who claimed to have slept with more than 100 women, possibly be just friends and nothing more with a 17 year old girl he knew from the internet? "You would be surprised" she said, "There's a lot more to him than you would think. Beneath his oh so macho veneer he has real feelings and real self confidence issues. He isn't comfortable being himself, that's why he has to be that exaggerated cartoonish version. It's all an act and what you see is what he puts on, it's almost all front."

"I know" I said, and then there was a pause. "So do you know where those marks on his arms come from?" I asked quietly, even though there was no-one else around to hear me.

She looked straight into my eyes, "yes" she said, "I do. He's been a bit down recently. And I know that it's not really my place to tell you, but, as you've probably worked out, he's not been happy for a long time and that's why he acts like he does. Believe it or not he's actually much better at controlling himself than he used to be. I've been to emotional depths with him and he's actually lost a lot of his self destruction." She sipped some wine and then elaborated, "I know that he talks a lot of shit sometimes and he gives you all of that 'wanting to feel alive' stuff, and in a sense it's true, he does. He takes the pills to help him find himself, but that's partially because when he's sober and alone and he has time to reflect he doesn't like who he is. He has an even lower opinion of himself than most people I know." She leaned forward, "You need to think of Brogan as a kind of sounding board for him and vice versa. She's young and she has all the of the same growing pains as every other middle class teenage girl, but he main point is that she listens to him and he listens to her."

"But if he has problems then there are people in the 3D world who can help him. If he came to me with a problem then I would do everything that I could to help."

"But he likes the anonymity, and that's what the internet is all about, you can be whoever you want in cyber space. I know that you think you can help him, and don't get me wrong you probably could, but that's not what he needs. He cares a lot about you, but when he looks at you he feels like you're from some kind of perfectly comfortable world and that you look down on him a bit because of how he is. He wants to feel like he can be himself but he's obviously too afraid. It cuts him up to think that he can't turn to people, and of course it's that same insecurity about what everyone else might think that causes him to loathe himself, and that's the reason he literally cuts himself up."

"I'm shocked and I don't really know what to say. But how much of this do you know, and how much of it is just conjecture? How much of it has he actually told you?"

"Most of it" she said confidently. "Of course some of it is inference, but you have to remember that I've known him a lot longer than you have. And it's nothing personal, but he finds it far harder to talk to men. He's been like this since before I knew him. At school he was the class clown and when he was a student he was always drinking, doping and trying to impress people, even though it made him look kind of desperate." She took another sip from her wine and peered down to the floor. "The marks that are all over his arm came from his last breakup. They appeared one morning after they had argued and she told him it was definitely over. Let's just say that if you think that the way you're handling Penelope is bad then you should have seen him after Mandy left him. He was such a mess that he was drinking alcohol with his breakfast most mornings and snorting cocaine most evenings, and that went on for a long time."

I didn't know how to react because I was genuinely surprised by what she said. I guiltily recounted my last conversations with him, I had been so rude to him about Brogan and so derogatory about the way he lived his life. Where I was having problems was that I simply couldn't reconcile the sensitive and vulnerable Steven that she was talking about with the same misogynistic Steven who told me that he couldn't picture himself being with a girl who didn't want him for his money. Then I thought about it some more and it seemed obvious that Steven didn't really hate women, he hated himself.

We talked about him until it was so late that she couldn't be bothered going home. She got up and used my shower while I smoked a cigarette and then made a couple of green teas and prepared the couch for her. I felt hollow and empty as I thought about Steven and all of the seemingly insensitive things that I had said about him. I also wished that all of my friendships and relationships could be as simple and honest as the one I had with her.

Chapter 18

It was less than 24 hours later and I was trying to relegate the funeral to the back of my mind. I was attempting not to think about it as I lay back in the long grass and the thin reeds with my toes idly dangling over a stream. For that moment my chaotic life had become a brief and sanguine picture of leisure; I had the beautiful Venus on one side and a small glass of fruity white wine on the other. It was a picturesque summer day that was ripe for relaxation. My sleeves were rolled up, the sun was beating down and giving some much needed colour to my pasty white face and I had the smooth and succulent taste of a Marlboro cigarette on the tip of my lips.

Everything was quiet and still, the only things broaching our near perfect tranquillity were the gentle breeze in the air and the chattering of the busy birds in the distance. The day had started well; I had woken up and had breakfast with a tired Janice who was still on my couch from the night before. Afterwards I caught up with lovely Venus, and after only a couple of hours on the road we were so far away from the big dirty city that we couldn't even pick up a phone signal.

***

Venus was wearing a daisy chain around her head and a dandelion behind her ear that made her look like she had just fallen out of the hippy edition of a corporate catalogue. As I looked at her I felt the same kind of fuzzy romantic feeling that

I hadn't felt for years. I genuinely enjoyed her company and the more time that I was spending with her the longer I wanted it to last. It was a big symbolic day for me - this was the first time I had gone outside London with anyone since my early days with Penelope. The location was new but there were certain aspects of it that would have been the same no matter where we were; the wine was sweet, the weather was great and her company was divine.

I peered over the top of my sunglasses and watched her as she rolled herself something to smoke. She looked great; she was wearing a short denim skirt, a cute smile and a skinny fitted white shirt that was just thin enough for me to see her nipples through it. For a few seconds I stared at them and thought about what she would be like in bed, I knew she would be good but I couldn't tell if she would be gentle or rough. I wondered how many men she had slept with, I hoped that it wasn't many, although I knew that there was no way that she could have ever been stuck for options. As I watched her rolling her tobacco I felt the immensely self-centred pride of a man who knows he's about to spend the night with a girl who all his friends would love to have sex with.

My misogynistic daydreaming was broken up by a lonely plane flying overhead; it was a reminder of where we had come from, and a reminder of how unusual it felt to be so far away from it all. We waved up at the plane, although I knew fine-well that wherever they were going it couldn't be as good as where I was. Over the last few days I had dreamt of going far away with her; I wanted to climb tall mountains with her, swim in deep rivers with her and hop from train to train and country to country with her. I imagined us spending far away summers hitch hiking around Europe and living off our wits, we may not have got that far yet, but we had made a great start.

***

After we finished the wine we took a wander through the hills. The beaten track was pretty well trodden, so it was clear enough to give us some direction, and the cracked cobbled old roads and lush green fields made for a beautifully peaceful stroll. The climbing was slow and easy, and when we got to the top we sat on an old wooden bench where we stopped for another cigarette and admired the view. There were no signs of cars or people for miles, and it was so nice to be somewhere where we couldn't see London. Beyond the hills and valleys we could see the sun slowly melting into the sea; it looked far more like a photo from a Mediterranean postcard than anything that you would usually associate with sleepy England. I held her hand in mine and with the other one I used my keys to carve our initials into the bench like they do in old movies. I rubbed her palm as we looked out across the horizon, there were splashes of pink and brown across a backdrop that was becoming gradually darker as the sun was getting closer to its bed.

The top of the hill was the first place that I had picked up a phone reception for hours. My Blackberry purred quietly in my pocket, it was nothing important though; my inbox was full of spam emails from fake sheiks and I had a missed call from work that could wait until we got back. With hindsight that missed call was my final chance to save myself from the horrible night ahead. Instead we went back to the hotel and my Blackberry fell into a deep sleep.

***

My first weekend away with Penelope had been a total disaster. I had been working a weekend bar job at the time and had managed to scrape together enough pennies to take her away to a secluded B&B just outside Oxford. There wasn't a great deal of class in my plan, I was a 21 year old virgin at the time and I was tired of wearing my unintended celibacy like a favourite jumper. My plan had been foolproof; I had packed a box of scented rose petals, candles, champagne and chocolates in a bag in the car boot before we had left. She didn't suspect a thing as I waited until she was in the shower to 'grab a newspaper from the reception'. In reality I was giving my bag of tricks to the receptionist, who I had bribed with £10 to turn our small cramped room into an elaborate romantic boudoir.

The next step of my plan was to get her out of the room. The problem was that after her shower it turned out she was in the mood for staying in. She sat wrapped up in the smallest towel I've ever seen and urged me to stay and let her massage me. I hadn't planned for this eventually, so I smiled uneasily and kept giving really bad reasons for why we had to get out. "I just want one cigarette" I said in what must have looked like the poorest excuse that's ever been given to avoid sex. She wasn't stupid, so she had trouble buying into the idea of me being so addicted to nicotine that I was willing to delay losing my virginity. So instead I tried plan B and told her that I had a surprise dinner reservation in a restaurant only a few miles away.

Now that I had found a romantic sounding excuse to delay the exact same thing that I was trying to build up to I merely had to stay away for long enough to allow the receptionist to work his magic. The restaurant idea was a bad one, it meant that not only did I have to buy dinner, but I also had to find somewhere in the area that we could go. The problem was that I didn't have a booking so I had to get into an argument with every waiter in town, who all quite correctly pointed out that they had never spoken to me and that it was a Saturday night so of course they were fully booked. In the end I apologised profusely as we sat on the boot of my car and shared a bag of chips.

When we got back I shot a knowing wink at the receptionist who raised an eyebrow and gave me a really unsubtle air high-five. After the disappointment of dinner I was really excited to see how the room would look when it had been custom made for intimacy and romance. As I opened the door it was dark and all I could see was the flickering light of my candles, so far so good. Penelope's jaw dropped, "oh Floyd, you didn't need to do any of this" she said with a look of positive surprise. For that short moment in time I felt like I must have been the best boyfriend in the world.

The bliss was to be short lived.

As we walked into the room I noticed the most horrendous smell, then I saw a trail of feathers all over the ground. My optimism completely died when I saw that the window was open and there were a flock of pigeons sitting on the ledge. "Oh for fucks sake" I muttered far too loudly. I walked over and shooed them away, but the damage had been done. There was pigeon shit and chewed up rose petals everywhere; it was all over the floor, all over the furniture and all over my otherwise perfectly laid bed.

I shook my head in disbelief, I couldn't figure out whether to laugh or cry. Needless to say we didn't have sex that night - instead we drove back to London and tried to pretend that our 'romantic weekend' had never happened.

***

This time the hotel was a bit classier. It was on a big flag waving country estate of a place that looked like a quaint throwback to a bygone era of devout Britishness and countryside manors, an age that I'm not sure ever existed outside the realms of fiction. There were pony treks that left from the front door every hour for the children and hunts for the parents, on top of that, and true to form, the manager himself was a fat, pompous, jovial fox-hunting sort of chap. He spoke with a naturally posh sneer and every time we saw him he was wearing a big Sherlock Holmes inspired deerstalker hat and was wrapped up in tweed.

The room that we were in (which we could only afford due to that great combination of a newspaper promotion and a recession that had dragged down prices) was probably the same size as my bedroom, kitchen, and bathroom combined. It looked like it had been designed for a really posh slumber party; it had a big chunky King sized bed, an en-suite Jacuzzi and an overflowing mini-bar that was loaded up with extortionately priced spirits and exotic wines. On top of that, the big shiny bathroom alone must have been worth more than the entire contents of my flat. The best part was that we had a big long balcony with great views of unblemished landscapes that stretched for miles.

When we got in we kicked off our shoes, then I lit a candle and let the sweet scent of incense infuse the air. Then I poured some more wine and put another bottle on ice. She smiled as I turned on the radio and put on some light slow jazz music. I did a few seconds of cringe inducing cheesy dancing and then slowly walked over and put my arms around her. She giggled as I lightly kissed her on the mouth. This was how my first weekend all those years ago had been intended to feel. All of the signs were good as I cast all of my memories of sexual naivety and innocent failure to one side and focused on the wonder of the glorious girl that lay before me.

My heart sped up a little bit and I felt positively light headed. This was exactly what I had wanted from the weekend. I felt so drifty and everything was so serene that the mood was perfect for me to look into her big happy eyes and say those three short, overused and incredibly destructive words...

"I love you."

Chapter 19

BOOM!

I was stunned. A shiver of anxiety shot through my entire body as I realised the enormity of the horrendous thing that I had just said. My face was now fixed in possibly the least romantic and most desperately contorted and pleading expression that I had ever pulled. I didn't even have an excuse, it wasn't as if I could put it down to alcohol or hysterics; on the contrary I had been incredibly calm and almost entirely sober when I had said it. I tried to regain some composure, but my nerves got the better of me and my automatic reflex was to blink repeatedly and gawk at her like some kind of idiot. I could feel my stomach cramping up with the same sort of horrific anticipation that you feel when you're going uphill on a roller-coaster and my nose started to tickle and tremble with fear like it had on so many embarrassing occasions.

Her response seemed to take forever. "Thank you Floyd", she paused uneasily, "I don't really know what to say." I managed to force a smile, but on the inside I felt like I was minutes away from having a fully fledged breakdown. I had no idea what to do so I kept looking at her awkwardly. I didn't know if I was waiting for her to put me out of my misery by reiterating my delusions or to wind me with a short and sharp emotional punch to the gut. She didn't do either of those things; instead she let her eyes trail to the ground and stepped forward, then she leaned in again to hug me.

I held her tightly. Her hug was like an emotional godsend. Tears of gratitude ran down my cheeks. I strengthened my grip as I ran my hands through her beautiful hair and lightly pressed my quivering lips against her head. "I love you." BOOM! I had just said it again. If there was any doubt about my new found fixation on emotional self-destruction then it had just been vanquished.

She slowly pulled out of the hug and walked to the other side of the room. She kept her head down to avoid looking at me. I felt pitiful and stranded as I sat down on the bed and watched her going over to the window. "I'm sorry", she whispered as she stepped out to the balcony. My defences were down and I could feel my face heating up. I started counting to 100 in my head, I desperately wanted to distract myself from the fact that I was in danger of getting yet another nerve induced nosebleed. I rolled onto my side and looked across the room, there were so many things that I wished for in those few seconds. I wished that the day had never happened and that I could go back to having wine with Janice the night before. Failing that, I wished that I could go back in time by even 30 seconds, and then I would have bitten down on my tongue till it was too painful and swollen to say anything stupid.

I sat up a little bit and sipped from one of the now irrelevant glasses of wine that I had put on the nightstand. I turned my back to her as I sat up and finished the glass in one large unsexy gulp. Then I rubbed my eyes with one hand as I poured another large glassful with the other. After taking a big sip I lifted my heavy head from my hands and forced myself towards the balcony. "I'm sorry", I murmured. I felt like I had perfected the Midas touch but in reverse; everything that I was touching was turning into shit.

"Don't be so silly", she said sympathetically. She turned round and slowly walked over to hug me close to her again. "Put your arms around me," she said soothingly, "I won't tell anyone. You just caught me a bit off guard. I was flattered but I know that you didn't mean it. It wasn't even a bad thing to say, it was just a bit unexpected." I lowered my arms so that they were around her waist as she cuddled into me again. "You didn't do anything wrong so you don't need to worry." We stood still for a while and the impact of what I had said finally began to fade. The candles started to flicker as she pulled away and looked into my eyes. Her smile was like a warm beam of familiarity, her mouth was beautiful and her eyes glistened like priceless marble. Our embrace turned into a kiss, which became a much longer and more meaningful kiss, and then she led me back to the bedside

She sat me down and perched herself on my knee, and then she tenderly kissed me on the mouth, our tongues met as our eyes closed. Then she climbed on to the bed with me and gently massaged my back, the tension in my shoulders started to dissolve as she slowly rubbed them. "I want you Floyd" she whispered in my ear, then she stood up and took a couple of steps back, and then she unzipped her dress to reveal the most beautifully crafted body I have ever seen. My jaw dropped like a teenage boy who had just seen porn for the first time, she looked unbelievable.

I was utterly transfixed as she sat back down on my knee and kissed me delicately. I was completely under her spell. She was definitely the one who was calling all the shots as she ran one of her hands through my hair and used the other to help me unbutton my shirt. She was smiling as she stopped to reach for the wine and took a sip, letting some of it run down her chin.

By this point in any mainstream version of foreplay I should have been getting ready for the sex that would undoubtedly follow, but this time nothing was happening. A slow tinge of panic spread through my body as I realised that despite my more than noble intentions I was doomed to failure. The disconnect between my penis and my brain was unwelcome and unusual, mainly because in my mind there was nothing I wanted to do more than to lay her down and have sex with her, but I couldn't.

I knew that she was waiting for me to take over, so I felt an immense pressure to do something. I leaned in to kiss her and ran my hands down her back and across the curves of her body. She bit down on my neck and rubbed my leg, but then she pulled away and looked at me as if she was waiting for me to get undressed. I felt like I was being silently assessed as I stood up to remove my jeans. I took them off slowly so that she might think that I was trying to set a deliberately measured and slow romantic tone, whereas in reality I was actually trying to help her by delaying her from her inevitably disappointing fate. I felt like a virgin soldier reluctantly going to war as I forced a painful smile. My ego wouldn't let me tell her what was wrong, so the only thing I could do was take a gamble. Inside I was saying a million Hail Mary's, which was somewhat counterproductive as I knew that God must have a billion more important things to do than help confused men with erection problems, but I needed divine intervention or some kind of miracle if I had any hope of performing.

I sat back down on the bed and smiled awkwardly at her. She smiled back at me confidently, and then she wrapped her legs around my waist to pull me nearer. I knew that it would only be a matter of seconds before she found out what was wrong. Below my tightly grinning exterior I was terrified, but what could I do? The mortifying fact is that the more I thought about how much I wanted it the worse it got, I could swear that if anything I was getting even smaller. "I want you Floyd" she whispered again. "Come on" she said, "let's see it" she whispered with a wink, and then she reached for it. I didn't know what else I could do so I playfully slapped her hands away. She thought I was just teasing her and playing hard to get, so she smirked and reached out again.

I batted her hands away again and hid below the sheets. As I lay under the quilt I thought about slipping out at the other end of the bed and escaping into the bathroom. The problem was that I couldn't think of a way to do it that would have looked anything other than ridiculous. Then she trapped me! She sat on top of the covers. I fought for my freedom but her knees were holding down my arms. I kicked frantically as she uncovered my scared face. I felt powerless and I could tell from her almost sadistic grin that she had me exactly where she wanted me. She kissed me on the forehead again and then ran one of her hands slowly down my tensed up body. I was beaten. I stopped the fight and bit down on the inside of my mouth as I prepared to go down solemnly like a captain onboard a sinking ship. Within those long and embarrassing few seconds I speedily tried to recount every single sexy image that I had ever seen or dreamt of, but it was no good.

This time she managed to touch it.

As soon as she did I saw a fleeting flash of disappointment in her eyes. She looked up at me sympathetically and then down at my sorry looking penis. After a few seconds the proverbial penny dropped and she realised that her exuberance wasn't exactly helping matters, so she removed her legs from my arms and kissed my cheek, and then she slowly pulled down by boxers. "It's ok" she said, "just relax." I closed my eyes and lay back self-consciously. I felt exposed and rigid. I knew that I should have been enjoying it, but it simply wasn't doing anything. I tried to play my part by imaging how good it would feel to have sex with her, but that didn't do anything either. Some of the things that I was imagining were the sexual equivalent of the storming of the Bastille, and under any other circumstances they would have got me totally in the mood, but somehow still nothing was even hinting at happening.

I was the most defenceless that I had ever been as I lay there prolonging our mutual humiliation. Everything that she was doing had been utterly fruitless, so she put it in her mouth and slowly sucked on it, but that didn't work either. I don't think I have ever felt the same level of discomfort as I felt while she tried out absolutely everything in her sexual arsenal. I knew that she was feeling self conscious too, but she couldn't have felt nearly as bad as me. After about 10 excruciating minutes she sat up and sighed. A short burst of sexual apathy crossed her face, she tried to disguise it with a smile, but it was too obvious. Within that split second I could feel myself being condemned to a lifetime of total inadequacy. I felt like I would never even be able to serve even my most primal functions ever again. I could feel my ego collapsing as I shook myself free and pulled away.

You may not believe me when I say this, but it had genuinely never happened to me before. I have numerous flaws and an unlimited list of inadequacies to fall back upon, but a faulty penis has never been one of them. Ever since my very first teenage fumbles and frolics I've been more than capable of staying hard, so what were the odds that the first time it would ever happen would be my first and only time with the most beautiful girl that I would ever have the chance to sleep with?

At first she was silent. I turned my back to her and sat on the bedside. I put my head in my hands and sat hunched up and tense like a big ball of OTT vulnerability. Venus tried to put her arms around me but I shook her off, and then she tried to talk to me but I wasn't listening. After a few minutes I got up from the bed and went to pick up my clothes. I felt terrible, but I was able to hold myself together just enough to refrain from saying anything really embarrassing. Despite that, I still couldn't bring myself to look into her eyes; I knew that if I did that then I would either get her condemnation or her pity. Her condemnation would have been hard, but her pity would have been almost impossible to deal with. There nothing worse than having people pity you, it just confirms that you're the sort of person who deserves to be pitied. I couldn't bear the thought of having her tell me about how 'it can happen to anyone' or any of the other nonsense that's somehow meant to be comforting.

I turned my back to her as I put my clothes back on. I rubbed my eyes again and then I buttoned my shirt up as I walked towards the door. She half heartedly chased after me and tried to stop me with a hug, but I easily fought her off with a small shove. While I pushed her away I saw that she was on the verge of crying. I asked myself what right she could possibly have to be so upset.

As I slammed the door behind me all that I could think about was how much I wanted to get out of that manufactured pit of luxury and head back to London.

Chapter 20

I went downstairs to the bar. At first I was simply going to occupy a corner and heal myself with some wine, but I knew that she would probably come downstairs to find me. I pondered my options as I bought a bottle of their cheapest Merlot. I decided that I wanted some time alone so I took it outside.

There weren't any benches outside and I was too drunk to drive anywhere. It was still quite warm though, so after scanning the horizon I decided to climb up the hill behind the hotel. It was an easy terrain, which is just as well because I was halfway up when I realised that it was much higher than it had looked, and I was even less fit than I had thought. When I reached the top I was somewhat out of breath, but I found the same old bench that we had carved our names into that afternoon. I smiled wryly as I sat down and cracked open my lonely bottle. The first sip was horrible; it was a cheap house red and it was unspeakably foul. I wanted to cover up the taste and cleanse my palate by smoking something, but when I patted around in my pockets I found out to my horror that I only had two cigarettes left. I didn't want to go all the way back to the hotel bar to get more, so I tried my best to ration them, but I wasn't very good at it and within 10 short minutes I had smoked them both.

As I surveyed my big dark kingdom I felt like I was the last man alive in a zombie film. There were no signs of human life for miles and miles and the vast swathes of countryside had never felt so apocalyptic and oppressive. In front of me there were wide panoramic views of absolutely nothing, it was like I was in one big barren hell-hole that was being sadistically stretched to breaking point. There was nothing to see except trees and hills, there were none of the sights of the city and none of the well controlled man-made beauty of the suburbs. I could see the odd light flicking on and off in the distance, but they were too few and far between to form any kind of pattern, they were the same kind of distant hubs of life as Sophie had grown up in, and I couldn't think of anything worse.

I could feel my phone vibrating gently in my pocket but I didn't want to answer it, I knew that it would be Venus trying to call from the phone at the reception. There was a part of me that was curious to see if I meant enough for her to come out to find me, but a much larger part of me wanted to hide from her for a little bit longer. I took another sip from the hideous wine, for some reason I was surprised to discover that it still tasted just as bad as it had the first time. I measured my options and decided to keep moving, so I walked into the valley on the other side of the hill.

***

I felt like I had walked for miles, although in reality I hadn't gone very far at all. My navigation was extremely poor though, and towards the bottom of the hill I tripped and scraped my knee on a big stray rock that had been hiding in the grass. I felt worthless and drunk as it threw me off my course and into the long grass. I hit the ground with a hollow thud and my mind went into darkness.

When I regained full consciousness my throat was dry and my body was tired and dehydrated. I had a splitting headache and when I looked down I saw a thick splash of red wine spilt all over my shirt. I stayed seated by the rock for a while and finished the bottle, before throwing it into a bush. I cursed myself for having finished my cigarettes, cursed the alcohol for making it impossible to drive away and cursed the countryside for killing my phone reception. I looked up at the stars, but they were just a blurry mess in the sky. The moon was big and bright though, and it almost appeared to be laughing at me as I lay in my impotent wine soaked heap.

I know this sounds stupid now, but in the back of my mind I could hear a deeper version of my own voice telling me that there was a chance that I might die out there. The voice kept saying that I was miles from home and that I was so far into the middle of nowhere that if I were to die then it would take months before anyone found me. My head was racing with a million bad scenarios and paranoid questions; how many people 'go missing' every day in the countryside? There were no signs of life around me, had anyone even been to this part before? Do you get wolves in England? I know that I was being irrational and stupid, but by that point my senses and my reasoning were pretty far gone.

I eventually managed to force myself up so that I could pee. I felt pretty clumsy, so I supported myself by leaning against a tree and peeing downhill, although in reality I can't imagine that much of it went any further than my shoes. I started to feel nauseous and sickly as the wind battered me against the bark. I couldn't take the wobbling any longer. I had to lie down again, so I lowered myself against it until my back was slumped in the reeds and my head was rested against the tough old stump. It wasn't comfortable in the slightest, but there was no way that I was going to be able to find my way back, so it was going to have to be my bed for the night.

***

I woke up in exactly the same place that I had crashed out. It was a bad start to the day to say the least; I felt hungry, thirsty and dirty, on top of that my head felt truly horrid and I smelt like I had decayed overnight. At first I was startled by the thick red stains on my shirt, to the untrained hung-over mind they had looked less like alcohol and more like the products of an open wound. My eyes squinted and adjusted to the morning sun that was poking through a big white cloud. There were no signs that anything around me had changed or that anyone else had seen me.

I used the tree that I had slept under to hoist myself up. I was dopey and achy, but I still remembered to stop and gather all of the things that had fallen out of my pockets. Everything was in good working order except for my mobile, which had now lost all of its power as well as its reception. My disconcertion came to an end with the sight of my empty wine bottle a few feet away, it was in the long grass next to the rock that I had gracelessly tripped over.

I felt really embarrassed and silly about what had happened in the hotel room, even though I had managed to upstage myself by passing out in a field. I knew that I had lost what would probably be my only chance to ever have a relationship with a girl as stunning as Venus. Despite that depressing thought I still managed to force myself to giggle at the fact that I had managed to ruin a romantic weekend by telling my girlfriend that I was in love with her.

As I stepped into the reception area the rest of the guests looked faintly horrified. A security guard started to approach, he looked really tough, but thankfully he backed off when he saw me taking out my key card. When I got back to the room I saw that she had left, then I looked at my clock and I saw that it was almost 10.45, so she had probably been gone for hours.

I needed to pull myself together, so I had a long shower and shave; I didn't feel the need to rush because I had already missed the complementary breakfast. After I got out of the shower I threw myself onto the bed. I was still too far over the limit to think about driving home and the room was non refundable, so I decided to get my head in one piece and stay for the rest of the day.

***

By the time I got home that night I felt a little bit better. On the way back I had made sure to drive extra slowly; I knew that if the police had stopped me then my license would probably have been revoked on the spot. As I re-approached the city my phone began to rumble with new messages. I had a missed call from Steven and a text from Janice that asked if I would be back for Sunday Night Wine. She said that she had some really good news, which was a relief because it meant that the focus wouldn't be on my 'romantic weekend'.

I decided to call Steven and tell him about what had happened, I thought it would be easier and less embarrassing to do it that way than to let him bully it out of me over wine. The call began with him telling me about his night, which had been spent at a club night called Happy Hookers, which sounded like possibly the most tasteless event in the world. After he had told me all about how he and a bunch of other professionals had dressed like prostitutes and pimps he asked how my weekend had gone. At first he was surprisingly supportive, in fact he almost sounded compassionate, which was nice because I had missed out the bits about me saying 'I love you' and focused almost exclusively on my biological malfunction. "So she left because you didn't have an erection?" he asked. I was happy to let him think that was what happened, he didn't need to know any more than that. "I'm sorry to hear it", he said sympathetically, "but don't worry, it can happen to any of us." Unfortunately his guise of decency could only last for so long before he decided that he couldn't withhold his urge to announce how much better he was than me. "Floyd, I have had sex with lots of people, and although I have never even once had a complaint, or any reason to question my abilities, but I know that far greater men than you who have had off-nights, but unlike you most of them wouldn't have the guts to admit it."

"Thanks I think. Anyway I'm not looking for your counsel, but I would appreciate it if you could keep it to yourself and avoid bringing up the topic of my love-life when we meet up tomorrow."

"Of course," he said, "and on that point, what do you reckon Janice's news will be?"

"I would suspect either a new man or a new job. I can't see it being anything else."

"That's what I'm banking on too. Nothing exciting ever happens around here. Anyway, ciao for now and I'll see you tomorrow."

"Sure thing mate, and thanks again."

"That's ok, your secret's safe with me."

***

I thought about whether or not I should phone her, but what could I say? I had gone from telling her that I loved her to walking out on her during sex, and all within the space of 10 minutes. To make matters worse, the fact that I had spent the night getting drunk in a field meant that she probably had to hitchhike back to London, so it was safe to assume that we weren't going to be dating any more.

I tried calling her, but unsurprisingly it went straight to her answer machine.

"Hi this is Venus; I'm away from the phone just now. Please leave me a message and I'll get back to you."

"Hi its Floyd, I know that you probably don't want to speak to me, but I'm calling to say that I am really sorry. You were probably expecting that but it's still true, I really mean it. Also, thanks for the part of the weekend that happened before I ruined everything. I'm starting to ramble, but I want to say sorry again. Oh god, this is getting awkward, but I really am sorry. Call me if you ever want to talk again."

That was the last time I spoke to her.

Chapter 21

That Sunday we met in a sleepy riverside bar that lay just outside the city centre. The atmosphere was pretty calm, but there was a sense of mystery in the air as we waited for Janice to break the unofficial 'no good news' rule. Steven and I had got there first and needless to say he had kept bringing up my 'issue' while we waited. He kept smirking at me between drinks and unsubtly trying to weave my malfunction into conversation.

When Janice finally arrived she was wearing a massive smile. "So guys, I have really big news" she said excitedly.

"Well whatever it is I have even bigger news" interrupted Steven.

"No you don't" she snapped.

"Oh yes I do, believe me."

"Steven will you shut up and let me talk"

"I was just saying..."

"Wait your turn then" she said, and then she stopped, she was obviously really excited about whatever it was that she had to tell us. She paused for a bit of dramatic effect and bit down on her lip.

"Well?" he asked impatiently.

"So guys, I don't quite know how to say this, but it looks like I'm going. I'm packing my bags and I'm finally leaving London."

ANTI-BOOM!

I felt a strangely hollow and underwhelmed sense of surprise. Her big announcement had somehow managed to be both a shock to the system and a massive anti-climax at the same time. It had definitely been a long time coming, but I guess that I had always assumed she would never leave. I had always thought of it as just being one of those things we talked about every so often but it wouldn't actually amount to anything. I didn't know what to say so my first response was an underwhelmed and unenthused silence.

She was confused, "so," she began slowly "which of you is going to be the first to congratulate me?"

"Congratulations" I said with an upset murmur. "I'm just a bit stunned. I mean wow, so what's happened? Where's your new home?" I asked with anticipation, although to be honest I didn't really care about how it had happened, I just wanted to scream "take me with you; I don't care where you're going."

"I've got a few plans kicking around," she said, "but it looks like I'm moving to Chester. I'm going to move in with April and chuck in finance to start working with her." She smiled, and for the first time since I've known her she looked genuinely happy. "So, what do you think?" I sat forward and attentively, I had adopted a confused smile, but Steven was yet to move, or to even express any feelings about it whatsoever.

I spoke first. "I think it's a tremendous opportunity and there's a huge part of me wishes that I was doing the exact same thing."

"Thanks Floyd," there was a thoughtful silence in the air as she smiled at me sweetly.

Steven had his wine glass pressed to his lips. After he had finished drinking from it he finally broke his silence. "I'm pleased for you, I really am, and this feels like it has been in the making for years. But despite everything we may say I just don't understand why you want to leave London. Can you tell me one thing that Chester's got that London doesn't? I mean you're in one of the greatest cities in the world. You have lots of friends here, you have a good job here and you have a life here."

***

The first conversation that I had ever had with Janice had been a very short one about the weather. It was one of those typically British conversations that began when I ran into her in the foyer one morning at work. We were both pretty soaked because we had been caught out by an April shower and neither of us had brought umbrellas.

She saw me dripping all over the floor as we waited, "It's horrible outside," she said flatly, I nodded and smiled. That banal moment of agreement was the first and last thing that we ever said to each other until some weeks later when we began working on the same floor. She had moved to an office only a few doors away from mine, in those days she was still an ambitious new analyst and a lot of influential people in the company were keeping a close eye on her. She ticked all the right boxes for a long and prosperous career; she had written an award winning undergraduate thesis, she came from a well connected family, and she had spent her summers doing internships for different banks all over the City. She was also pretty bullet proof because she had a simple but well meaning sense of integrity; she wasn't driven by any illusions or love of the industry. She wasn't even driven by the money, instead she was driven almost purely by a desire to be successful in her own right, and she thought that finance was the best vehicle for her to do it.

We became friends through sharing short five minute chats in the kitchen when we made coffee. Over time our short snippets about films, books and TV shows extended to lunch time conversations and then to drinks after work. We became friend pretty quickly; I liked her brashness and assertiveness, and I guess that she must have liked something about me. To be honest I think she was relived as I was probably the only man at the firm who wasn't trying to hit on her or belittle her every time I spoke to her. There was a short fluttering few days when Colin had flirted with the idea of making her my line manager, but it never came to anything and he awarded the role to Sophie instead. The fact that it was ever even on the cards shows how different Janice and I used to be; she used to stay late every night and bring mountains of work home with her to do over the weekends while I tried to get away with doing nothing. The transition that she made between that and being another card carrying member of Generation Debt was the product of being overlooked by our bosses one time too many.

I remember the first time that she introduced me to Steven, partially because it came with a health warning. "I have a feeling this might be a big mistake" she said, "but he's one of my best friends and I think you'll like him." She had been friends with him since before she moved to London, they had both gone to the same University, and had both finished top of their classes, even though his student experience had been somewhat more hedonistic than hers. Although I had never met him I had heard lots about him, he was somewhat notorious. He had been brought in by Colin as some kind of protégé, Colin was attracted to his ruthlessness and saw him as the exact sort of person he could work on like a pet project and mould into a future leader. Then the crash happened. Steven's decline into Generation Debt was neither born of disillusionment nor apathy, it was almost entirely accidental. When the crash happened Colin had to stop micromanaging him, and with his boss out of the picture Steven no longer felt like he had to impress anyone. His previous work experience had all been based around student politics so that was the mindset he regressed back into. He stopped feeling pressurised into being the next big thing in finance and instead concentrated on socialising and drinking.

Sure enough, the first time I met him I hated him. On the face of it he had every bad quality that I had spent my life trying to avoid in my friends, but he also had an irritatingly magnetic quality about him and every time we met I became slightly more immune to him. There were also lots of perks to being his friend, it meant that by proxy I was friends with Colin, it meant that I got to drink in slightly better pubs and it meant that other people assumed I was slightly cooler than I was. It might sound contrived but being seen to be slightly cool was important to me. Now that the trickledown effect has been eradicated and replaced by a banker lead pursuit of individual glory then the race for cool is almost all that Generation Debt has left.

***

"Thanks guys," she said as she sat back down, "I really mean that. The last few years have been great, and we have been through so much together, but I feel like it's time for me to move on. I've always said that I would never stay in a job that made me unhappy, but that's what I've been doing for months now."

"But why can't you work for a charity in London?" asked Steven, "Everyone in this city needs help, I mean look at the people in this bar, we all look nice and middle class, but that's all just a charade. This city is the most messed up of them all, if we aren't popping anti depressants then we're snorting coke. Besides if it's poor people you're interested in then there are lots of tramps around here."

"But it's not just my job I want out of, it's London too. I'm sick of all of the noise and I'm sick of getting into work every morning smelling like a dirty commuter. I'm sick of all of the personal politics and the bullshit that goes with finance. I'm sick of practically coughing up my dirty lungs every day because of the fumes and the pollution. I'm sick of paying an extortionate rate of rent to live in a glorified shoebox and I'm sick of getting ripped-off every time I go to a shop." She took a sip from her wine and thought about what she had just said. "I'm sorry and I know that I'm sounding really bitchy and spoilt, and I know that it's not all bad. I'm glad that I've had the chance to live here, and I'm glad that I've had the chance to live among the lights and the glamour, but I won't miss it when I'm gone." She paused for a moment "I will miss you guys a lot though, you're my best friends, and you've always been there for me."

She was right; the three of us had made a great team. I genuinely felt like I might become rudderless without her; she had been like the well grounded rational ying to my neurotic anxiety ridden yang. She continued, "I just feel like I've given this place so much of me and I've received such little in return. The city just keeps asking for more, and then it leaves us chewed up, washed out, loveless, and lost. It's done it to so many of us, it's done it to me before, and if I don't leave then it'll do it again."

"London doesn't have to be like that, it's big enough to be whatever you want it to be," said Steven, "It can be the worst cesspool on Earth, or it can be a massive party. People from all over the world flock here for a reason, they flock here because they see the opportunity that's available and because we have the best shops, the best clubs and the best parks. We are the fashion capital, political capital, social capital, and media capital of Europe. Of course it's busy and of course parts of it are rough and dirty, but it's a city. I can understand why you want to leave, but you're not choosing to leave just anywhere, you're choosing to leave London."

"You're right I am choosing to leave London, it might not be forever, and maybe one day in the far future I'll have a yearning to come back, but it isn't right for me at the moment and I don't think it ever will be. No city should ever make you turn to anti depressants and wine to stop from crying every night, and this one does. I know that Chester might not be the greatest or the trendiest place in the world for a night out, but it just feels so much better for me right now."

An unplanned silence took over the scene. We all tried to ignore it. Steven went to the bar, Janice checked her Blackberry and I couldn't think of anything else to do so I pretended to tie my shoelaces. It was the comment about anti depressants that had done it, we both knew that she took pills, but it was something that we only talked about in private, and now that she has said it in our threesome it made it seem more official.

"So what's your best London memory?" I asked in an attempt to get us away from the pills.

She thought about it for a few seconds. "I don't know, it's probably a combination of my first week here, which was when I saw the museums and everything, and I felt like a tourist, or it's one of our Sunday nights."

"What was the worst?"

"Probably the time Steven and I had a bit too much to drink and he ended up staying over." She raised her eyebrows, as if she were daring me to believe her, but before I could say anything he came back from the bar with a fresh bottle of something red. I smiled to myself as he refilled our glasses and sat down.

With my mind still focused on the question of whether or not they had slept together I stood up. Despite my distraction, I had a mix of hope and despair in my voice as I lead in raising my glass. "Janice, Sunday night wine won't be the same without you, you're a great friend and we'll miss you. To Janice."

"To us", she said as our glasses met in the air.

We didn't say anything for a while. "So what was your news Steven?" she asked.

"Nothing," he said smiling, "it's just that Floyd can't get an erection."

I think that last sentence sums up both the banality and the banter that went hand in hand with Sunday Night Wine. That was the last time we did it, and I hope that we can do it again.

Chapter 22

By the time I got home I was slightly drunk and emotional. It was wet outside so I was also soaked. It had been pretty dry when I had set out, and so as per usual I had decided that I was far too manly for an umbrella, only to see a bunch of far more manly men than me walking around with umbrellas, hats and scarves. The rain didn't really bother me though; I had my iPod, so I spent the walk listening to Tori Amos and recounting my favourite memories of Janice. As I walked in my front door I was thinking about the time when we had gone for a long weekend in Canterbury and visited all of the sites from her favourite childhood books. My nostalgia was interrupted by my Blackberry. It was Sophie, I had no idea why she was calling and it was nearly midnight but I took the call anyway.

"Floyd, I think that it's time we sorted a few things out, are you at home?"

I looked at the clock, I really couldn't be bothered seeing her. "No, I'm out."

"Where are you?" I was stumped, where could I say I was on a Sunday night at 12?

"I'm just out."

"No you're not", she said, "Your bedroom light's on." BUSTED. "I'm outside, and before you say anything I'm not stalking you.

I spent the night with friends in a bar around the corner, just let me in. Don't worry, it won't take long." She hung up. She must have been close because it was only a few seconds later that the buzzer went. When I opened the door and let her in she shot me a look of anger and frustration, it was one of those 'I don't know why I bother with you' sorts of looks. Without saying a word I took her jacket and umbrella and hung them up in the hallway while she invited herself through to my lounge.

I left her alone for a couple of minutes while I put the kettle on in the kitchen, if we were going to talk about awkward things then at least we could do it over something warm. She takes her coffee black, it's one of the things that we have in common. By the time I brought it through she was sitting on my couch. For a couple of seconds I thought about sitting next to her, but instead I decided to make it obvious that I didn't want to be speaking to her, so I sat on the battered old chair at the other side of the room. "So what's on your mind?" I asked, as I put down the drinks.

"You're very far away," she said with just enough hostility to make me feel a couple of feet smaller. "Anyway, we haven't spoken in ages and people are starting to notice. I've got so much to do and I don't want another week of us trying our best to avoid each other. So I want you to tell me, where do we stand?"

I tried to play for time by taking a sip of my coffee, but it was far too hot so it burnt the inside of my mouth. I tried not to make it too obvious that I was in a great deal of pain as I put it back down. "I don't really know", I said, "We're still friends aren't we?" I paused. "Look, I know that I owe you an apology. I'm sorry for everything that's happened, it's not really much of an excuse but everything's been so hectic recently and I haven't really been thinking straight."

Her confused eyes met mine, and then she shook her head, "you weren't thinking straight? Is that all you can say?" For fucks sake Floyd I'm supposed to be your boss. You can't simply walk all over me, trample all over my emotions and then just say sorry and then that's it. How can we just pretend that nothing happened?" I could see the start of a tear in the corner of her eye, and then she put her head in her hands and hunched forward to cover her face.

I didn't know what to do, should I have gone over? Should I have put my arm around her and comforted her? I was too gutless; instead I stayed glued to my seat and fumbled with my mug. It was still far too warm, and every time I took a sip it seemed warmer, but I had to drink it because that burning hot coffee was my only sanctuary from her grief. I knew that none of this was her fault, I know that she's hardly an angel, but the only reason she felt like she did was because of me. It wasn't as if I hadn't been warned about what might happen, Steven had warned me repeatedly, how could it possibly be the case that I had been so wrong, and yet he had been right?

"I'm sorry", I choked out, I knew that I sounded insincere and uncaring, but I didn't know what else I could say, and the only reason I even said anything was to break the silence. I knew that there were probably more eloquent words that I could have used, but I had no idea what they were. In books and films people always come out with the perfect lines, but it was real life and I had already fallen into a mumbling mess before I could think of anything smart to say.

She reached for a tissue and blew her nose really loudly. She looked at me through a small break in her fringe, her eyes were wet and blurry and her makeup had started to run. "You're an ass hole Floyd. Despite my better judgement you actually made me care about you."

I shrugged harshly, I felt completely incapable of saying anything right, so I didn't even try. "I thought it was just some fun," I said, without anywhere near enough sensitivity.

She looked away as I crossed the room and sat next to her on the couch. There was a pause before I stretched out my arm; I did it slowly enough so that she had a choice about if she wanted a hug. She didn't even look up, she just slapped it away. "Don't you dare touch me", she hissed quietly. I pulled my arm back as she curled in to the other end of the sofa, she was as far away from me as that little couch was going to let her get. "I've had it with people like you," she muttered, "when you look at me all you see is an easy girl with a big ass, well I've got a brain too." She stood up, "I know that you're one of the people who think that I only got to where I am by sleeping with Colin, but that's bullshit. There's far more to me than the things that all of those liars say, I got here because I worked hard."

We had all heard about how Sophie had come from a broken family, and about how she had left school at 15, and about how she had come down to London from some quiet village in the midlands. We all knew that this was her story; it had been repeated over and over in company memos and press releases when she became a manager. The problem was that none of us bought in to this version of her so none of us could make any sense of it. If we listened to the 'official' back-story then she had magically transformed from a rural wannabe artist who spoke in poetry to being a City bound power slut who dreamed in HD.

"I don't know what you've been through", she said, almost spitting out each word, "but if the world has slapped you around then it's kicked the hell out of me. I'm not from some metropolitan middle class suburb like you. I come from alcoholic parents, a rough house with a broken roof and the kind of former mining village where everybody uses drugs and nobody has a job. You don't know how hard it was for me to avoid falling into a life of mashing baby food and peeling potatoes by the time I was 18." She turned to go, "I'm leaving", she mumbled, "I don't want to stay here for another second."

There were tears in her eyes as she put on her jacket. I stood up again and trailed a few steps behind her as we went to the front door. We didn't say another word, or make any more eye contact, until she was out of my front door. "You know that if I was the great big bitch that you think I am then I would fire you on the spot and make sure you never worked again." I nodded.

I went to my window and watched as she left the front door. She was hiding below her umbrella, she walked through the puddles and rain and towards the train station, and she didn't look back once.

Chapter 23

Janice's leaving party was a disaster. It was on a Wednesday night and it was an awkward time of the year so there were only a handful of us who could make it. Steven and I were there, but the rest of the guests were either people I didn't know or people that I would never normally have chosen to socialise with. To throw in a bit of spice and controversy the star attraction of the night was her mother.

I was curious about meeting her, but it was in the same voyeuristic and morbid kind of way as I would be curious to meet a cannibal or a serial killer. I had heard lots of stories; I had heard about all of the rants about her carelessness, her insensitivity, her callousness, and the way that she always had to control everything. I was expecting her to be a stern and sour faced old dragon, so when I met her I was surprised because she didn't look anything like I had expected. She was really small and quiet and what stuck out for me was her closed off body language, her lack of social skills, and her sexless demeanour. It hadn't been a great party before she had arrived, but it got a lot worse when she did. Everything became a bit tense as we all stopped paying attention to each other and started watching her through the corners of our collective eyes. Her gloom was contagious, it wasn't as if her being there had merely changed the atmosphere, in fact she had sucked the life out of it. She hadn't actually been invited, she had called Janice the night before and asked if she was having any celebrations, after a ton of emotional blackmail poor Janice's defences had crumbled and she had finally caved and told her that she was welcome to pop by for a drink if she wanted to.

***

Her last few days at the office had been really quiet, there was no work to do and we just spent time smoking on the step outside and wishing we could be somewhere else. "So what happened with you and Venus?" she asked, "was Steven telling the truth when he said that she dumped you because you couldn't get it up?"

"No" I said with a smirk. "It was because I confessed my love to her and then I tried to have sex with her, but I couldn't get an erection so I ran outside with a bottle of wine. To make up for it I got really drunk and slept in a field." She covered her mouth and tried not to make it obvious that she was laughing, but I could tell that she was.

"I suppose that's one sure-fire way to ensure you don't see someone again."

"Tell me about it, so much for a romantic weekend."

"So why did you say it? Did you love her?" She was trying her best to sound serious, but she was still grinning.

I bit my bottom lip and wondered whether I should respond seriously or not. "No I definitely wasn't in love with her," I responded with a shrug. "But she was cool and I enjoyed hanging out with her."

She laughed sympathetically and then put on a mock sad face. There was a short pause. "So why have you been acting like such a penis recently?"

I laughed because her directness had taken me by surprise. "Truthfully, I don't know, I used to think I knew, but I'm not sure that I do anymore. I used to think that it was because of my breakup. But that doesn't make sense because I was acting like a penis when I did it, not just afterwards."

"Why were you so scared to turn 25?" she asked.

"I don't know" I mused, "it just felt so final and irreversible. It felt like there could be no way back and it's not long before I'll need to know about pension schemes and mortgages and I'll have to start thinking about the rest of my life."

"What are you talking about? Being 25 isn't old at all."

"Yeah, but it's too late for us to be thinking about reinventing ourselves or starting new careers, not that there would be any jobs even if we could."

She threw away her cigarette butt and lit up another one. "But reinvention and new beginnings are exactly what I'm trying to do now. Do you know that I've never said the words 'I love you' to anyone?" she took a draw. "Except for my parents when I was too young to know what it meant, and if I could retract having said it then I would in a heartbeat. I've never been in love."

***

That was the memory that was imprinted on my mind as we sat in her stairwell finishing the last of the wine after her party. The night had been memorable for all of the wrong reasons. Her mother, who had drank a little bit too much, chose that night to unload 25 years of built up resentment on her youngest daughter. "Why do you never call me without prompting", she asked spitefully while Janice was taking an arm full of jackets through to the cupboard in the hall. It wasn't a very big house, so as soon as I heard the tone of her voice I ushered both of them through to the bedroom so that people would be slightly less likely to hear what was going on. The impact was negligible; the walls were thin enough to ensure that we could all hear everything. Everyone had stopped talking so that they could hear the argument. Our jaws were collectively dropped as it reached its crescendo and her mother screamed at her. "Why do you always have to be such a stuck up little cunt?" she bellowed as she threw her glass onto the ground.

From that point onwards the party was officially over, it went on for another half an hour or so, but none of us were going to forget that we had just seen our friend's mother drinking too much and dropping the C-bomb. To his credit Steven was the first to act, and as soon as it was dropped he called a taxi and practically carried the old witch downstairs. Janice was mortified and stayed in her bedroom whilel tried to shoo away the other guests.

After the gaggle had gone Steven and I stayed in the lounge and finished what was left of the snacks. We munched on Hoola Hoops and M&Ms until she eventually came back through. She was trying to make herself smile, but she was visibly upset, she was shaking and her eyes were like charcoal because her tears had smudged her makeup. She hugged us and whispered a thank you, and then she sat down with a cigarette. Steven went to get her some coffee and I gave her another hug.

"This is awful," she said. "It was only a few nights ago that we were having our final bottle of wine, and tonight has been yet another example of just how much I've come to depend on you guys." She took another puff on her cigarette and shook her head. "You know that I'm kind of glad it's just the three of us left, I didn't really want any of the others to be here anyway. I only really invited most of them because I wanted her to think I was popular."

***

Her departure itself was something of a logistical failure. She had gone for a coffee with Steven that morning for their goodbye, and I had taken an extended lunch break so that I could see her off at Euston station. I had formulated one of those perfect monologues in my head but everything seemed to work against me and I found myself delayed by overcrowded streets and an inept underground system. When I eventually got to her platform I was 20 minutes late and extremely stressed, but I had managed to make it just before she left. It was an oddly repressed goodbye; we didn't really say a lot, the big things were implicit and the little things could remain unsaid. We simply shared one last long hug, and then I kissed her forehead and helped her to carry her cases onto the train.

I waved from the platform as she pulled away. Her face was practically pressed against the window in a slightly panic struck half smile. I wished that I could have arrived in time to give her my monologue. I would have told her that she had been like the sister I never had and that whatever happens to her in Chester I will always love her and will always be thinking of her. I wanted to tell her about how grateful I was for everything that she had done for me, and how much I was going to miss her.

Chapter 24

It was a few days after she left that my department were given half an hour's notice of what was our first all team forum in years. These meetings used to happen every eight weeks or so but we hadn't had one since the start of the crash, so we all knew that it would have to be something serious. My colleagues and I were silent as we trooped down to the main hall. For the last few weeks all of the trade magazines and newspapers had been running stories based on rumours that Colin was on the verge of a breakdown, so it was a distinct possibility that he had called the meeting to announce his resignation.

We were all surprised to see that there was a group of large, externally hired mercenary-like security guards at the door to go through our pockets and check our ID cards. They looked pretty uncompromising and tough. They had a register of everyone who was allowed in, they had obviously been told not to talk to us because they barely made any eye contact and none of them made any attempt to put us at ease.

The group who had been called in before us were leaving at the same time as we arrived. Their faces were etched in a state of collective shock. I wanted to stop and ask them what happened, but I couldn't because the security wouldn't like it. I gulped as my mind focused on only one word, CUTS.

Very soon the room was filled to capacity as Colin, Sophie and a couple of their yes men took their seats on the stage. They were separated from the rest of us by a row of the meanest looking, storm-troopers that I've ever seen outside of riot footage or documentaries about the Gestapo. The room fell into an anxious silence as a sound system at the back of the hall began playing Fidelio and Colin stepped up to the podium. He gave nods of familiarity to a couple of people who were dotted around us and gently waved the guards down from their aggressive stances.

Despite his entrance music and the show of force he still looked terrified. It was obvious from his body language that he wanted it all to be over with as soon as possible. His eyes were grey and motionless, but his face was given away by his sweaty forehead and a bulging blood vessel that ran between his eyes. He had never been a very hands-on Director so the great majority of the people staring at him must have been perfect strangers. I had only ever met him at occasional team building session s and staff daytrips, but they had been few and far between. Somewhere along the line he had become a small scale celebrity and was now one of the least popular public faces of a sector that everyone hated.

Since the crash his family had been forced to move out of town and live with an army of around the clock bodyguards. He wasn't just hated by the protesters though, his constant desire for the spotlight had seen him trying to engage in almost every single public debate on monetary policy and in doing so he had managed to frustrate and alienate most of the industry.

There was a time when he would have loved to be performing in front of a room full of his adoring employees. In the old days, when the gravy train was in full swing, he would probably have invited the media and turned it into a ceremony to celebrate his own greatness. But it was obvious from the security all around us and the sleepless look on his face that this wasn't going to be one of those occasions. He took out a notepad that he had scrawled messy notes all over and placed it on the podium while he put his reading glasses on. He knew that we were all expecting bad news, but that didn't stop him from delaying things a bit longer by pouring himself a glass of water and checking his phone for messages one last time. He shot a glance over to Sophie who nodded, as if he needed her permission to speak, and then she looked down at her own notes and tried to avoid further eye contact with anyone else in the room.

"I want to start by thanking all of you for coming with such short notice," he said slightly hoarsely. "I know that there's been a lot of speculation in the media and I want to nip it in the bud. I love this company and contrary to any of the stories that you may have heard I'm not going anywhere." He paused, he had clearly allowed space in his script for applause, but nobody was going to be clapping their hands until we had heard why we had all been called together. "We are a great company" he said, "and the reason that we have become a market leader is not because of me, it is because of us and because we are the best. Our turnover this year has been better than almost anyone in the sector, we are one of few major companies around here that are still expanding our services and taking on new graduates, and the most important thing is that we haven't needed a bailout." He paused again, this time he took a long sip of water. His eyes were now fully focused on his notes. He forced a cough before he started reading out a long list of awards that we had won.

"Get on with it" shouted a solitary angry voice from the middle of the hall. He stopped mid flow and looked to the guards, who quickly returned to a more confrontational stance. He shook his head slowly as if to say 'you've just made a big mistake.' After a few seconds of suspenseful silence he returned to reading his list, although this time he finished uninterrupted. "So why have I asked you all to come here today?" he asked himself rhetorically, "the reason is because I believe that you need to hear this from me and not through the grapevine or from the media." He stopped reading his notes and slowly scanned the room to measure how well he was doing with his jury of dependents. "As you are all aware, we have found ourselves in a sea of financial problems and we need to turn our sinking ship into an agile canoe if we are to ride out this storm. None of this is your fault, in fact all of this is despite your hard work and in no way because of it. You are my dream team." He stopped again; he could feel the collective confidence of the room dropping. "There are a lot of people who would love to shut me up for good and to shut us down for good, but I won't let that happen. However, despite their attacks we can't exist in a vacuum, and unfortunately if we are going to save ourselves then to do so we have no choice but to trim down our operation. The Board has tied my hands, and the investors and shareholders have ensured that their hands are tied too. None of us want to be doing this, but we will need to let a number of you go during the weeks and months ahead." The guards could sense a growing restlessness among us, so they raised their fists accordingly. "The original target that we were set was to downsize by 10 percent, but all of the indicators say that this won't be enough." There was a hostile call out from a trade unionist at the back of the room, Colin nodded in the direction of a security guard who grabbed the poor guy and dragged him outside in a scene that looked like something out of a tyranny. "After a long meeting this morning with my American counterparts I have had to ask Sophie and her team to find savings of between 17 and 20 percent" there were gasps from the floor. "I know it's harsh, and I don't like doing this, I know that it's horrible, but it's the only thing that we can do if we are to survive in this climate."

There was no vocal resistance this time, nobody wanted to be the one who raised their voice and jeopardised their future. I tried to read Sophie's body language but it wasn't saying a lot, she was writing lots of notes and trying to avoid making any obvious or emotive gestures. She must have known that I would be looking at her. I had seen how strained she had been only a couple of weeks or so before, so it was utterly implausible that she would somehow be alright about it now. I remembered back to her big pile of rotas and the red pen that had been all over them, none of this was sounding good. I didn't really pay much attention to anything else that he said, I just kept my eyes fixated on her, I wanted to see if she would show even a flash of the same sincerity and weakness that I had seen before.

Finally he stopped. There was no applause, everyone was far too worried. We all felt like we had taken a collective shot to the head. It was made worse by the fact that thanks to a number of newspaper articles we all knew exactly how much money he was being paid for doing it. There was no time for any questions; he walked off stage into a safe backroom with Sophie and a couple of corporate hit men. There were some murmurs, but most of us stayed silent as the guards opened the doors to let us out. The next group was already waiting in the foyer, but nobody exchanged a word. We knew that they could tell exactly what was coming.

Within a few short minutes we had gone from being colleagues to being rivals. The union members all went outside for an angry post mortem and a cigarette. I decided not to go with them, it would seem a bit opportunistic of me when you consider that I had never done as much as read a single one of their pamphlets. The union didn't really fight for people like me anyway; their membership was almost exclusively made up of security guards, cleaners and admin staff.

I caught up with Steven, he was pretty worried too, but in the back of his mind he felt more secure because of the fact that he got on reasonably well with Colin. The problem is that friendships don't really mean a lot in the City, at least not outside of the top 5% of the company, as he would soon find out. The point that worried both of us was that the top 5% of the company accounted for one third of all wages, and that meant that in order to cut our costs by 20% without losing them then we would probably have to lose about one third of the rest of us. The problem was that most of us were too selfish to be thinking about defending each other. I remembered how I felt when Sophie had fired those janitors, I had felt guilty for a couple of hours, but the guilt was nullified when I had found out that George was alright. I had barely even passed a thought for the ones that weren't so lucky.

That night I tried to phone Sophie but she didn't reply. I knew that she would be screening her calls but I hoped that the part of her that liked me would convince her to pick up and let me know what the odds were that I was going to be fired. After my third attempt I stopped trying, it was obvious that she wasn't going to speak to me. It was two hours later and I was in bed that she eventually got back to me with a sarcastic text message, *'I can't think why you've phoned me three times tonight... I'll see you at work tomorrow'*. I couldn't sleep that night because I was dreading what was going to happen. I had no doubt that Sophie's text messages and phone logs would now be added to some kind of dossier outlining why I should be the first to go.

Chapter 25

I couldn't think of any reason for them to keep employing me ahead of anyone else. To be honest almost anyone else would have put more effort into the job than I did. It was an odd pickle to be in, because on one hand I knew that the worst case scenario was that I would lose my job, yet somehow the idea of escaping from an environment that I hated still seemed like a bad thing. I had kept looking out for Venus and George, but I hadn't seen either of them. Venus was so new that she was still on probation, so it wouldn't be hard to get rid of her. As for George, he was a morbidly obese cleaner who could be replaced at the click of a finger, so it didn't look good for him either.

I tried phoning Venus to see if she was ok but the call didn't even ring before it disconnected. I wasn't doing it because I thought she would have forgiven me, I was doing it more dutifully than anything else. Even before I called I knew that there was almost no chance of her picking up. I was stuck in a moment of self doubt and panic, so after a lot of consideration I also tried phoning Penelope so that I could hear her familiar voice, but that didn't work either. When I called her mobile it was actually her dad's voice that I heard.

"Yes?" he barked.

"Hello" I mumbled, "Is Penelope there?"

"As a matter of fact no," he said sternly. "Is that you Floyd?"

"No" I said, although I knew that he would see through me.

"Good" he said with emphasis, "because if you were him then I would ask you not to phone back. She has a new phone and that's largely because of what he did to her." I gulped, "but as you're so clearly someone totally different then I won't tell you any of this, will I?" on that point he grunted and hung up.

***

Penelope's dad never really liked me. It's not that I'm classically bad boyfriend material; I would say that I'm actually relatively nice, decent, respectful and honest. The problem was that the first time we met I was a bit too honest. The first time I met him was when both her parents popped down to London for a long weekend. They hadn't been down for years so they were spending an afternoon doing touristy things before coming round to our house for evening tea. I was extremely nervous about meeting them because it had already been such a long time coming that I felt like I could only disappoint. Penelope and I had been living together for months and she was a regular at my family's BBQs and Sunday lunches, but somehow I had managed to avoid hers.

Penelope had never been close to them when she was growing up, and in fact she had gone through almost every single stereotypical stage of teenage rebellion. When I had met her she was on the way out of 'punk' phase that had involved lots of hair dye and The Sex Pistols, before that there had been bouts of paganism, heavy metal music, left wing politics and light drugs. The rebellion was a cover for her middle class upbringing; if my parents were a bit well to do then hers were practically aristocracy. Their dysfunctional relationships and personal complications were compounded and amplified by their regular visits to long expensive 'family therapy sessions' in which they were all meant to learn about how to tolerate one another.

I had met her brother a few times, but we never really clicked. There was always that unshakeable overarching awkwardness which was born from the fact that I had slept with his sister. What are you meant to say to your sister's boyfriends? Are you meant to be friends with them? Does the whole sex thing always have to get in the way? I know for a fact that if I had a sister then I would undoubtedly be the most overbearing and overprotective brother in the world. I don't trust young men or teenage boys because I used to be one, so I know how they think. Thankfully parents are usually able to overlook these things, or at least they force themselves to piece together mental pictures of traditional courtship, romance and grandchildren born from celibate means.

I was on my best behaviour when they arrived. I had ironed my shirt, tidied the house and shaved especially for them. We got off on the right foot because it turned out that in one of those classical small world types of scenarios her dad used to work in the same building as I did. He was a former investment banker who still has his fingers in lots of corrupt financial pies, and he was still very well off because he had hidden a lot of his money in offshore accounts and given up the rat race shortly before everything had gone to the wall. He had lived across the social spectrum, having grown up as the son of a rural shoe-shiner he had become a city slicker, before retiring into the role of a country gentleman. Despite the lifestyle that went with it he had never liked the City, but he was very ambitious and very driven, and as an unreconstructed Thatcherite he defines everything exclusively in terms of its monetary value. In contrast her mother is a very nice, even if somewhat subordinate, woman. She has never had much to complain about and hasn't had to work since she gave up on a promising teaching career to become a full time housewife and mother.

I knew that they would be expecting big things from me so we had choreographed almost everything to perfection. As soon as the car pulled up I turned on the kettle while she ran out to see them. I arranged a selection of biscuits and teas and took a tray through to greet them with. "This is Floyd" she excitedly explained to her flustered mother and her cheerful looking father. I reached out and shook his hand then I leaned over to hug her mother. We had one of those slightly awkward half hugs where neither of us could tell whether or not we were going to do it or not until we were half way through.

Penelope took their coats while I showed them around. It only took me a few seconds to guide them through our humble little flat, so I focused on the views and pointed out the landmarks on the city skyline.

As we all sat down Penelope and I pretended to be engrossed as her dad told us all about how much the area had changed over the last 20 years. Then we had to sit through lots of photos from their afternoon, they were just like any other city centre photo collection and included the usual round of pictures of them smiling outside the South Bank Centre, Piccadilly Circus and Buckingham Palace.

The first stage of my cross-examination was quite gentle. They asked a few softball questions about what the area was like and what train connections I used to get to work in the morning; it was really just banalities before they got to the real meat of their questions. During the second stage they asked me lots of things about my background, which was fine and acceptable because it was middle class, so I passed that stage too. The final stage was when they asked me about my job; they wanted to know exactly what I did and what sort of things I could see myself doing. It felt like everything was going really well, her mother kept giving me approving looks, especially when I told them about how much I earned and how much I could expect to earn if I stayed at the company. Both figures were totally exaggerated, but they had been chosen in order to paint me as a safe and reliable pair of hands. The signs were good, and when I went to get another round of teas I pressed my ear to the kitchen door and heard them telling her about how nice I seemed.

It's no exaggeration to say that everything had been going brilliantly until we played Scrabble...

It was after our third round of tea that we suggested they stayed longer. Her dad was a board game champion at his local village pub, so we decided to facilitate a bit of introductory bonding with a quick game of Scrabble. Penelope and her mother fetched the game and scrambled the letters while her father and I discussed politics, economics and the ways of the world. It was one of those classically one sided male conversations in which he provided the wit, wisdom and insight and I sat in glowing admiration.

When Penelope and her mother brought through the game we stopped out of politeness and he gave me a knowing and respecting nod. I smiled at him in a way that suggested we had just shared a private joke at the expense of the doting women in our lives. "What were you talking about?" her mother asked with a mocking curiosity, he tapped his nose and we both let out over the top laughs, this was all going too well to be true.

While I was chuckling I fished my hand into the little green bag and pulled out my seven letters. I laid them out in the order I plucked them: L A N I G A V. This is where it all went wrong. Her mother, who was sitting on my right, began the game with the word SALT. Then Penelope, who hadn't got any vowels, changed her letters so it was my turn next. I looked at the board and then at my letters, and that's where I saw that if I arranged them backwards then I could connect my V to the T in salt to spell TV and use the rest of my letters to spell the word VAGINAL. It was a valid word, but could I bring myself to put it down? When I studied the board I realised that there was a double word score on the L, which meant that if I did it then I would get 72 points.

I knew that it was a risk, so I took a minute to weigh up the various possible outcomes in my head. It was a bold predicament that could either end in awkwardness, anger or hilarity. In my head I could hear Steven urging me to do it, "go on Floyd, what's the worst that could happen? It's a valid word that has medical connotations. They'll realise that it took balls to do and that'll show them that you're not a flake. If you do it then they're bound to respect you." I could also just as easily imagine Janice telling me the exact opposite. "Don't do it Floyd, it's far too risky and it'll just remind them that the last vagina you saw was their daughter's." I stopped considering if it was right or not and instead I tried to think about the numerous legitimate contexts and interpretations of the word vaginal. The only thing that I could think about was the phrase vaginal intercourse.

All of their eyes were on me now. There was a growing impatience in the air so I felt rushed to decide. "I'm not meaning to be rude" her dad said rather rudely, "but if you don't have any words then you can swap some of your letters."

"No, I've got one" I said hesitantly as I scooped them all up and placed them down slowly to spell it out: VAGINAL.

At first no-one said anything, then a few seconds later her father broke the peace. "Vaginal" he said loudly and slowly, as if he was trying to remove any doubt about what I had written. I nodded solemnly. No one laughed or smiled or even commented on the fact I had just got a double word score, instead they looked at me with a very English mixture of prudence and fear.

The rest of the game was played out in near silence. My cheeks were burning with anxiety, and every time I looked over at Penelope she looked even more mortified than she had before. When we eventually finished I had won by 65 points, which was almost entirely down to the 72 points that I got for vaginal.

***

When they left her dad gave her a hug and a kiss, but didn't even make eye contact with me, her mother did the same. As I watched them driving off I could tell that the first thing they would comment on was my ineptitude.

As soon as they had gone Penelope slapped me. "Why the hell did you do that?" she shouted.

"I'm sorry" I said nervously, "but I didn't think it would be such a big deal, and it was worth 72 points."

"How could it not be a big deal?" she shouted. "Their first impression of you is that you're the sort of person who would put down the word vaginal in order to win a game of Scrabble."

She went through to the lounge and slammed the door behind her.

***

Although I never made that same mistake again it did condemn me to a disposition of chronic sycophancy which saw me trying far too hard to convince them that I was alright. I was so desperate to make it up to them that I would overcompensate with badly acted laughter every time one of them ever told a joke in my company. I spent hours rehearsing 'clever' things that I could say in front of them, but none of them worked. The problem is that there are few things on earth worse than people who are constantly trying to be impressive. I must have looked pretty tragic by the 10th time I had said something cringe-inducing like "you guys are such a perfect couple, so it's really no wonder that your daughter is so lovely".

They never met my parents, which is a shame because I think they would have got along, if for no other reason than the fact that her dad is everything that mine has always aspired to be. I kept suggesting to Penelope that we should do the whole 'one big family' type of thing, but she could read between the lines and she was never enthusiastic enough to get around to arranging anything. The Scrabble wasn't the only reason we didn't click, the major aspect of it was that when the novelty wore off they thought that I was pretty average. It was always obvious that Penelope wasn't going to be working around the clock in any kind of financial environment, and I think that by the time I met them they had carved out a vision of her being a stay home mother for a rich husband, and they just didn't see me as that rich husband.

Chapter 26

A few days later I was sitting at my desk and numbly looking across the skyline. Everything looked so bleak; the sky was gray, any daylight that penetrated the clouds was being choked by pollution and there were 'for sale' signs on almost all of the houses and shops in the area. The protests and confrontations may have stopped for a few days, but the signs of the most recent skirmishes were scattered across the streets and there were gang tags all over the walls of a lot of the banks.

The civil war that was going on around us had been escalated over the last few days when a gang of protesters had gone to Richmond Park in the dead of night and set a fire. I had watched the flames from the roof of my stairwell, the fields were ablaze and the streets were chaotic as fire engines from across the city were being called out. Despite the time it wasn't long before news channel helicopters encircled the scene and began blasting live images into the sitting rooms of the masses. After a while I went back downstairs and watched it with a sense of bewilderment. The last few months had seen protests but nothing like that, and until that night Richmond had been one of the last places you would expect to see any trouble.

That morning there had been even more gossiping in the corridors than usual, Colin's house overlooked the park, and no one had heard if he had been affected by anything that had happened. It turned out that he was fine; he had been away over night in one of our European offices. There was a sense of collective frustration when we heard that he was coming back to London because we all knew that he would be meeting Sophie to discuss the review.

The process was still in its infancy but it was the only thing that anyone was talking about. Steven was still feeling more confident about it than I was. He had managed to have a one-to-one with Colin who had apparently done all but promise him a promotion once the cuts were over. I knew that my situation made me particularly vulnerable so I felt around 90% sure that they were going to get rid of me.

My default position had become one of total apprehension. I was wearing my stress as if it were a favourite jumper; it was all over my face, and over the last few days I had been too anxious to eat properly. It was obvious that I couldn't begin to relax until I had spoken to Sophie. I knew that my future with the company was entirely dependent on her, so I had to know what she was thinking.

I tried calling her office but there was no response, so I went upstairs to the canteen in the hope that I would pass her on route, unfortunately I didn't, but I did get a disgusting coffee. As I drank my coffee I reflected on the fact that I was now in the exact opposite position from only a few weeks before when I had been desperately trying to avoid her at all costs, now I was desperately trying to run into her. My train of thought was soon derailed by the rasping sounds of two people kissing at the table next to mine. I shuddered with distaste and hoped that I had never looked that repulsive when I had kissed anyone in public.

I didn't want to stay there for lunch, so instead I went out to a local branch of Pret, where half of the office were buying sandwiches and speculating about who would be the first to go. I knew that all of their eyes were on me, the people who knew that I wasn't seeing Sophie anymore all thought that I would be first against the proverbial wall, and the ones who didn't know all thought that I was the only one who was safe. Over the last few weeks as the rumours had been spreading I had been getting a higher profile, it still wasn't high enough for me to get invited to social events but it was an improvement from total anonymity. I tried to get small talk with some of them, but the tone of conversation was almost universally bleak and the downbeat consensus appeared to be that we were all screwed.

The unions had already started balloting for industrial action, but nobody in a position of real responsibility wanted to strike, it would have just been an invitation for them to sack us. The only thing that we could do was to keep our heads low and hope that we got through it.

As I ate my sandwich I tried calling her mobile but it just rang until it went to her voicemail. I didn't want to leave a message, so instead I called one of the secretaries and tried to book a meeting with her under a different name. "Is she expecting you?" asked a stressed out receptionist while I explained that I was a long lost school friend and she would really appreciate it. I was amazed when my half baked plan worked and I was told I could see her for 10 minutes at six o'clock that evening.

***

That afternoon something very bad happened. When I got back from lunch I saw an ambulance parked outside with somebody being taken away on a stretcher. I couldn't make out who it was because they were covered in blood soaked towels and surrounded by paramedics. A crowd of people were looking on, there was a worrying air of indifference as everyone was shocked but no one was sad. I found a somewhat bemused Steven and asked him what had happened, "mate, you missed the shit hitting the fan" he said with a bit too much of a smirk to have really cared while he recounted the salacious details.

The man in the stretcher was George, but not many of the people who were gathered outside knew his name. He had been given his redundancy notice that morning and had tried to kill himself shortly afterwards. I was disgusted by Steven's heartless tone as he clearly revelled in telling me about it, but he was far from the only one, everyone else was gossiping and some people were even taking photos. Apparently he had locked himself in the toilet and tried to slash open his wrists with a pen knife. He was rescued by one of his colleagues who had heard his screams and broken down the door. Thankfully the knife wasn't sharp enough and he had missed the correct entry point, and although he had done a lot of damage and had lost a lot of blood it wasn't enough for it to be fatal.

I was shocked, and I felt a hideous numbness creeping through my body as I thought about him. Forget about the rest of us, George was the real embodiment of the collateral damage that goes with corporate greed. People like him are suffering at the coalface of our county's excess at the same time as cabals in boardrooms are plotting and scheming against the rest of us while giving themselves increased dividends. He had been fucked up to the point of self destruction by a cruel, heartless system, and the only thanks that he received for having spent his prime years on his hands and knees cleaning other people's piss was to be fired as part of a cynical drive to install greater confidence among a small clique of millionaires.

I thought about the humiliation and the helplessness that he must have felt to believe that dying could be better than living for another second. When someone like George, a career cleaner on a pitiful wage, is made unemployed it won't be easy for him to walk into another job. People like him are the last ones to be thought of during a recession, but always the first to be punished. As I watched him being driven away in the ambulance I wished that I could have been there for him. I walked away from Steven and went to a quiet little garden near the office, where I put my phone onto silent, smoked a cigarette and just sat with a chilling feeling in my bones.

I couldn't help thinking about the last 10 minutes before he did it, what had been going through his mind? If he had found out at the start of his shift then he would have worked for a further five hours, would he have known straight away that he wanted to do this? Was it something that he had been thinking about for a long time, or was it more impulsive? George had never hurt anyone, and he didn't deserve to be in a stretcher. I couldn't help but think back to the time that I had shunned him in Trafalgar Square because I didn't want Venus to see me talking to him, what had I been scared of? Considering that I thought of him as a friend and had cast him to one side so that

I could impress a girl, then it was no wonder that a crowd of strangers had been so detached from his suffering.

***

Sophie's office felt even more intimidating this time around. The last time that I had been there may have been awkward but this time I had just seen George being taken away in an ambulance and I knew that I would be grovelling for my job. Even at my most optimistic I couldn't conceive of any scenario in which she didn't fire me at the first chance she got. It wasn't that I had suddenly become enamoured by my work, but I didn't want to be unemployed, the economy was still in stagnation and I didn't fancy my chances of getting a good reference and being able to beat the 20,000 Generation Debt graduates who would probably be applying for every single vacancy.

I knocked on the door and waited until she shouted before going in. She must have already figured everything out because she didn't look at all surprised to see me. Instead she looked quite stressed and disappointed, but it was the kind of disappointment that comes from being proven correct. A hostile silence hung in the air as I closed the door behind me and walked over to her desk, where I stood and looked at my feet until she indicated that I could sit down. She didn't start any small talk or offer me any wine this time, she just stared blankly at me until I forced myself to open the conversation. "I'm really sorry to have dropped in unannounced" I said sheepishly, "but I need to know what's going to happen, are you about to fire me?"

As I said it I realised how stupid my plan was, if by any miracle she had decided that she wanted to keep me then this would almost certainly make her reconsider.

"Floyd" she said sternly, "the board has asked me to help them to make big cuts, and I would be making them irrespective of what may or may not have happened between us. Anyway, at the moment I'm looking at how we can offer voluntary severance packages and cut our administration costs, I haven't even begun to look at your department." She ran her hands through her hair before she rested her chin in them, "I'm not going to promise anything to anyone, but this isn't a witch hunt and I am certainly not going to be firing anyone just for the sake of it."

"Oh" I said flatly. There wasn't a lot that I could add, I didn't trust her at all, but it had always been naive to think that she was going to announce a grand plan to dispense of me while I was in her office. Now that I had just embarrassed myself I wanted to get up and leave, but I knew that having cheated my way into the meeting I had to stay, leaving would have made me look even worse. I didn't have anything else to say so I just sat in a silent trance as if I was waiting for her to keep talking. She looked directly at me which made me cast my eyes back towards my shoes.

"I'm sorry about everything that's happened between us" I said in an attempt to offer myself up as an emotional bastion of decency.

"Floyd", she snapped, "I don't want to hear it. None of this is helping either you or me, can't you see that the fact that you're even here is totally inappropriate? I have a lot to do so if you haven't got anything else to say then please go." It felt like I was back at school, it was like being told off by a particularly patronising teacher but I wasn't in a position to object. "My world doesn't revolve around you" she added. "There are over 5000 people working here, there are lots of them that I don't like, but that doesn't mean that I'm going to play office politics with their lives. I know that every red line on a sheet of paper represents someone's livelihood and that's a responsibility I take seriously."

"What about that cleaner who tried to kill himself today because of the redundancy notice he received?" I asked, trying to catch her out.

"Yes" she said slowly, "I did hear about that, and it was very unfortunate, but he also had a history of depression and mental instability. He wasn't made redundant by us, he was here as part of a government welfare to work scheme and the funding for it dried up. If the government were still willing to pay their portion of his wage then we would have matched them."

She had just silenced me again. I didn't know about any history of depression that George had, but I also had no reason to doubt her. I wanted to say something really clever or insightful in response, but my mind was blank. When she was contented with my subordination she stopped looking at me and tried to get back to what she was doing. After a few seconds I could tell that she was getting annoyed with me being there. She turned to face me again, "Floyd" she said slowly, "there's not really a nice way for me to say this, but can you please fuck off?"

As soon as she said it I got up, my legs had started to shake but I was able to hold onto the chair. I didn't want her to know how I was feeling so I forced a ghoulish smile to cover up my discomfort. I was particularly worried because I was starting to feel the familiar tingling pre blood sensation in my nose. As soon as I felt it I turned my back on her and left as quickly as I could.

By the time that I got back to my desk the trickling feeling had become a light flow and I had to go through to the bathroom to clean myself up. I sat on top of the toilet until it had stopped. I looked at myself in the mirror and felt pretty repelled. I didn't like the stray gray hairs on my head or the yellow bags that had formed under my eyes. My stomach felt heavy and worried and my mind was everywhere, I could feel a horrible sickliness building inside me as I thought about what was going to happen next.

***

I spent the night looking through the job pages of a couple of trade magazines and one of the local newspapers. There was nothing too exciting; it was just the usual toxic mix of things that I was overqualified for and things I could never do. I smoked a cigarette and put my feet up while I watched fresh pictures of the protests outside as they unfolded on the news.

Chapter 27

"Are you alone?" Steven whispered into my phone.

I took a long exhausted look at my clock, which said it was well after midnight, and then to the depressingly empty pillow next to me. I was dazed and confused as I mumbled something that must have sounded kind of like a yes. "Good," he said "because I'm coming round. Hang on for two minutes and I'll be right there", he hung up without elaborating any further, which left me feeling really confused as I rubbed my tired eyes and fumbled for my bedside lamp. My buzzer went off a few moments later, and to make sure that I responded quickly he held it down until I answered. "Finally!" he muttered after I had eventually managed to drag myself over. "Now hurry up and let me in before someone sees me, I don't have any time to explain."

"What the hell are you talking about?" I asked with an exhausted yawn, but he didn't say anything. "I was asleep until a couple of minutes ago" I mumbled as I dozily reached for the button to let him in. I opened the door and ran my hands through my hair as I leaned against the wall. I could hear him running up my stairs three or four at a time so I went through to the kitchen to wash my face in the sink, and then I grabbed a couple of cold beers from the fridge.

When he made it upstairs he came in panting and covered in a thick layer of glistening sweat, he was clearly knackered. He had big black bags under his eyes, he smelt vaguely of wildlife and he looked like he had spent the night sleeping in a bush. I knew that he had to be feeling rough so I gave him a sympathetic smile, but he ignored it and walked into the hallway as I closed the door behind him. I gestured with my eyes for him to go through to the lounge, which he did without saying anything. I let him sit comfortably before I broke the silence. "Okay" I said slowly as I walked in behind him, "so what the hell happened?" He looked at me and shook his head with obvious regret while I sat next to him and opened both beers with my key ring.

"Floyd, I'm sorry about the time, but I couldn't come any earlier, I promise that this is serious and that I'm not messing you around. I need you to listen, because I have just done something really, totally and utterly fucking stupid." I was getting worried. "Something bad happened tonight. It was just as I was about to leave for the day," he said, and then he stopped to take a quick drink. He looked favorably at my foreign beer and then returned to his story. "Anyway, it was about 6 o'clock and Sophie called me into her office. She didn't let me know what it was about so I thought that it may have just been because she wanted to bitch to me about you or something like that, but it wasn't. When I saw her she was in no mood for small talk, she just asked me to shut the door and sit down. She began by giving me some long-winded crock of shit about how good I am, which made me rightly suspicious as she turned it into a management-speak heavy monologue. Anyway, to cut a long story short she ended by telling me that despite everything she had just said she had no choice but to make me redundant."

"Oh my god" I said with disbelief. I was actually really shocked, not only because Steven was quite good at his job but also because he got on reasonably well with most of our bosses and I could think of about 100 people (me included) who were far more deserving of redundancy than him. There had been a time when Steven had been on the verge of entering the closed circle that advised and empowered Colin. He was invited along to client lunches and he had been taken to every corporate jolly and golf tournament on the go. That changed after the crash when power got even more centralised and the exclusive circles got even more exclusive, but we had both assumed that when the books were balanced he would be right back in there. "I really am sorry to hear that. I mean what the hell? Are you totally and 100 percent sure that it wasn't some kind of misunderstanding?"

"Definitely not", he said, "but needless to say my instant assumption was that she couldn't be serious. I thought that she might be bullshitting me, I thought that it might be one of those stupid corporate loyalty tests or something, so I laid on lots of compliments and argued my case. I verbally embraced her and told her how much I respected her. I complimented the hell out of her business acumen, and then I pointed to my own impressive record and told her that if she got rid of me then she would be making a big mistake. I had been so utterly fake and complimentary that I felt like if it was a test then I must have passed with flying colours, but she didn't mention any of it. All she could say was that it wasn't personal and that there was nothing that she could do about it anyway because the decision was out of her hands."

"That's really shitty" I said. I was still startled and although I knew that I wasn't exactly helping I didn't know what else I could say.

"It was totally shitty. Anyway, at first I didn't believe her, so of course I demanded to speak to Colin, but she said that it wouldn't do me any good because he was well aware of what was happening." He paused for a drink while he thought about what he wanted to say next. "I'm not going to lie, that part hurt me, because as you know I've always thought Colin and I were friends. We used to hang out quite a lot and I thought that there was at least a mutual respect between us, but obviously not. Although I knew that it was true I still wanted to hear it from him, so I told her that I wasn't going to go anywhere until I got to see him." I moved to the edge of the seat and prepared for the worst, I was already very worried about where the story was going. "Anyway she said that he was busy, but I wasn't going to accept that. So I stormed out of her office, having just called her a 'stupid fucking bitch', and marched upstairs to his room."

"Oh Jesus" I said quietly, "what did you do?"

"Well when I knocked on the door it was him who answered, so I marched in and shut it behind me, then I asked him flat out if it was true or not. He must have been expecting me because he didn't look at all surprised. He nodded calmly and told me that yes I was being made redundant. He said that he regretted it and that after things had calmed down he would hire me again. It was all of the same bullshit that he gives everyone else when he gets rid of them. I don't know why I had expected any better from him, but I had. Like I said, I always thought that he liked me. Anyway, I wasn't in the mood for taking any of his crap, so I told him where he could stick it. But then he got all defensive and gave me some crap about how he knew that it was shit but that's how business works."

"Please say that you left it at that" I said with a hint of desperation in my voice.

"Of course not", he scoffed, "I couldn't just accept it. My pride wouldn't let me walk away and let him think that he had got one over me. Anyway, you know what I'm like, so of course I ended up reacting in the stupidest way possible." He looked away from me so that he didn't have to make eye contact as he told me the rest. "Needless to say I got all in his face, and then he got in mine. So I started shouting and then he started shouting and it just kind of escalated from there. After a bit of verbal to and fro he shoved me, it wasn't even a hard shove, but I overreacted a little bit." He turned away in embarrassment about what he was going to say, "I took a swing and punched him hard in the face."My eyebrows shot up. "And then to make it even worse I head-butted him, and I'm pretty sure that I broke his nose."

I was in a state of stunned silence. All of us had fantasised about beating up Colin, but none of us had ever had the balls or the inclination to actually ever go through with it.

"So anyway, as I did it I could hear a loud cracking sound, and then he screamed, and then Sophie and a bunch of security guards threw open the door and burst into the room. They must have thought that I was armed or something."

"Oh my god," I murmured.

"At first I was in a state of shock, so I was just fixated on him, and he didn't look scary anymore. In truth he looked totally pathetic, and there was a stream of blood pouring from his nose and all over the carpet. They all started coming towards me, and I got pretty scared. I knew that the security guards could beat me to a pulp. So at first I tried to reason with them. I threw my hands up as if I was trying to surrender, and then I kept shouting at them that I was really sorry, but they were continuing to circle in, and I didn't think that they were going to go lightly on me." He took a sip of beer, "so what else could I do? I ran for it. I went for the smallest one of them, who was still a big bastard, and I charged at him with such force that I practically went through him. I punched him square in the jaw and kicked him in the shin, which worked because he had a weak leg and I made him bite down on his tongue. I had an extra few seconds to escape as he hobbled around like a pirate. Then I threw open the door and took to the stairs." He took another sip, "I'm not totally stupid though, I knew that the front desk would be guarded. So I went for the fire exit and ran until I found one of those bike hire stands, I got one of them and cycled to Kings Cross where I got on the tube. I didn't come here straight away though, when I got to the station I called Kenneth and we went for a few drinks in the pub round the corner in case anyone from the office came here to look for me."

"Wow," I said as I drank from my bottle. "I don't really know what to say."

"That's ok, but what the hell am I meant to do? There goes my job, there go all of my references and there goes my career."

"Mate," I began, although I was still too shocked to sound comforting, "it's not like that, I know you, and you'll sort it out."

"No I won't" he said, "I've fucked up everything, what kind of nut-job breaks the nose of a FTSE100 Director? You can get locked up for that sort of thing. Who on earth would want to hire me now?"

I genuinely didn't know what to say, so I let the question hang in the air for a few seconds before I changed the subject. "Do you know if they called the police?" I asked.

"I don't know" he said, "but I doubt it. They care too much about their PR to let the press print a story about some idiot doing something that everyone in the country would love to do. Not after what happened to that cleaner, it might give people ideas."

"You're not an idiot," I said. "And you're right, you did what a lot of us would love to do."

"I know, and for that split second when I could hear his nose snapping it felt so fucking exhilarating. I just thought take this you heartless fucking bastard, how can he treat anyone like that?"

I smiled at his sentiment, and then there was a heavy pause. "So what happens next?" I asked.

He took a big long sip of his beer and shook his head wearily, "I don't know. I've always been a bit confused, but right now I have absolutely no idea about what to do. You've seen my bills. There's no way that I can be unemployed for more than a few days, otherwise my house is going to turn into one big payday for the repo men."

I gave him a wry smile and offered him a cigarette, he took one and we both lit up as I got up to get an ash tray over from the window ledge. I had never smoked a cigarette that tasted so flavourless. I thought about how the few friends I had at work were all disappearing. First of all Janice had gone, then George lost his job in the most tragic way possible, and now Steven was sitting on my couch having just broken our boss's nose.

"Is there anything I can do?" I asked after a few more seconds of silence. "If you need for me to talk to anyone or you need a loan or anything then all you have to do is ask."

"No mate, nothing like that," he said, "I couldn't do that." He took a long draw from his cigarette. "I wish that Janice was still here," he said as he looked vacantly at the smoke. "She would know what to do. She'd have come up with some sort of solution by now. I just wish that I could think of one."

"I don't think there are any quick-fix solutions for something like this" I said. "Maybe it's just one of those crappy things that happen and you need to deal with it. Maybe it's one of those times when you have to re-evaluate everything and think about what you want to do with the rest of your life." I knew that I wasn't being hopeful or particularly constructive, but I also knew that he had totally fucked up.

After another few seconds of silence my phone vibrated on the coffee table, I looked over and saw that it was Sophie. I looked at him and raised my eyebrows. He looked over anxiously, but I shook my head to say that I wasn't going to answer it. I glanced out the window, I could see the demonic office block that she was probably calling from, and it stood out on the horizon like torchlight in a blitz. She tried a second time, but I still didn't answer, then it went off again, but this time it was a text message, *'I'm assuming that you haven't heard from Steven yet, well if you have (such as if he's round at your house right now) then please remind him that he is fired. X'* he looked over nervously, I nodded to say that it was exactly what he was expecting, he nodded too and took another nervous draw from his cigarette.

"You know what? I can't tell you how great it felt when my head connected with his nose, it was fucking brilliant." I laughed and we raised our bottles in jest. Then the loneliness of his position set in. "So what are you going to do when they decide it's your turn to go?" he asked after a few seconds of empty silence.

I shrugged my shoulders, "I'll try to say 'yes sir' and 'no sir' and do everything that I can to make sure that I get a good reference and as good a severance package as I can. Beyond that I don't have a clue."

"Does it scare you?" he asked.

"Yeah, it does. Are you scared?"

"Yes" he said, "I'm absolutely terrified." I leaned in closer so that I could give him the option of a hug if he wanted it, but he pulled further away, as if to say that I was already too close. "It's the sort of thing that you always expect to happen to someone else but never to you." He shook his head at his own naivety, "I don't want people to know that I've been sacked, it'll make them look at me differently, and I don't want that. I can't deal with that, I'm not someone who needs pity.

"You weren't sacked" I stressed. "You were made redundant. We're in the middle of a recession and it can happen to anyone."

"I just can't help but think that it shouldn't be happening to me. I preferred it when the only people who were affected were the cleaners and skivvies. What the hell am I going to do with my life?"

"Maybe it's an opportunity" I said, what do you want to do?

"I don't know. I used to think that I wanted status, money and the chance to live and work in London. I had all of those things until this morning, and now I don't know what I want anymore."

He stayed until the next morning. We didn't talk a great deal more about it.. He was sad and angry, but most of all he felt stranded, work isn't just what you do, it's also a part of who you are, and now that his job was gone he had lost a lot of what made him feel special. He was someone who was used to finishing on top of everything, so he wasn't used to being replaced or to finding out that he wasn't indestructible. Despite all of the tensions and the turmoil in the economy he had barely even prepared himself for the remotest possibility that he might be one of the ones to go, and now that it had happened he didn't know what to do.

The following morning we had a big cooked breakfast as I tried to help him to prepare for the next chapter in his life. I told him that I was planning on visiting George in hospital later that day. I asked him if he wanted to hang out until I went, but he said he didn't, instead he was going to go home and call Janice and Brogan to help him to figure everything out. I felt bad about the fact that he didn't feel like he could talk to me about it anymore, but I felt even worse about the fact that one of the only people that he felt like he could talk to was a 17 year old girl from the internet.

After he left I got ready to go to the hospital. I felt uncomfortable because I didn't know all that much about George, but I felt like if I didn't take a couple of hours to see him then no-one else would. By that point I had already resigned myself to the fact that I was soon to lose my job. When Steven had lost his he had inflicted violence on his bosses, and when George lost his he had inflicted violence on himself. I didn't know how I would handle it when it eventually happened to me, but I also knew that I was running out of people who I could turn to when it did.

Chapter 28

Before I saw George I met his mother. I don't know what I was expecting, but what I saw was a harsh and overweight world-worn woman who looked like she was on the wrong side of 60. She smiled gratefully from her bedside chair as she saw me approaching, then she said something to him and stood up. She opened the door and joined me in the corridor "Thank you for coming by" she said meekly, "this will mean so much to him. I've tried my best but I think he's bored of just me and the doctor." She leaned in and gave me a quick hug and a small peck on the cheek, "Can I get you some tea?" she asked.

"That would be good I said", she nodded and walked down the corridor. I felt very sorry for her as I watched her go. I knew that George's father had been a deadbeat who had disappeared when he was a young, and I knew that he didn't have a lot of friends at work, so aside from her I must have been among the only people that he had.

As I walked in he turned round with a surprised smile, I raised my eyebrows slightly uncomfortably and sat down next to him. He looked really bad, his gown was too small so it showed off just how pasty and overweight he was, and his face looked doughy. Because of how he was sitting his breathing was extremely slow and heavy. My eyes were drawn to his arm, which was hidden below a messy pile of bandages and tubes. The room itself couldn't have felt more sterile; the TV was off, there was no music, and aside from a couple of 'get well soon' cards and some second hand history books by his bedside there were no signs of any visitors. I wondered if either of the cards were from Colin or Sophie, but I didn't want to ask him as I was fairly confident that the answer would be no. "How are you doing?" I asked with a smile as I handed over a bag of grapes and a big old book about the history of the Labour Party.

"Thanks" he mumbled. He didn't make any eye contact with me, but he looked approvingly at the book. There was an uneasy silence in the room. I was hoping that he would take the lead in conversation because I didn't know what was ok to talk about. I didn't even know if I was allowed to acknowledge what had happened or if I had to pretend not to know. When I looked at his depressing figure I thought about how he must have felt during the last few seconds before he had sliced his wrists. I didn't know enough about him to know if he had a history of self harming, but I hoped that it was a one-off.

I looked out the window as I waited for him to say something. His room overlooked a busy main road, so it was really noisy and the view wasn't very nice. "Thanks for coming to see me" he said. "I'm sorry if my mother was a bit overbearing, she doesn't mean it." I smiled sympathetically and assured him that she had been fine. I didn't know a lot about her, George had always painted her as a kind of crazy old crank, but that image was totally at odds with the polite and grateful woman who had just gone to get me a cup of tea.

The silence returned, but this time it was slightly thicker and more intense. George knew that I wanted to ask him about his arm and I thought that he wanted to talk about it too, but a combination of fear and cowardice meant that I wasn't prepared to make the first move. Finally he did, "I know that everyone at work must have been talking about what happened" he said. I didn't respond but the implication of my silence was that he was right, "and I'm sorry if you were upset, but I was just so angry."

I tried to look into his eyes, but he didn't let me. "I heard about what happened", I said, "and I also heard that you had been made redundant, and I'm so sorry."

He shrugged, and then he looked down at his arm, "I didn't ever think that I would try to do that to myself. It's not something that I had even thought about before, but what you need to understand is that my entire world had just collapsed." He was being a lot more open than I had expected and I didn't know how to respond. I'm not a psychiatrist so I didn't know if it was a good idea for me to talk about it or if that would make him more likely to think about trying it again.

A few seconds later his mother came through and put down two cups of tea. Then she started moving towards the empty seat on the other side of the bed, but something must have clicked in her head and she turned around and left without saying a word. After the door shut he continued. "After I lost my job I realised that I don't have anything. My mother says that I'm special, but she's deluded, I mean look at me, I'm hideous." He stared at the roof with a look of despair, "I'm a fat minimum wage virgin. I've just lost my job and there's not a lot of work out there for someone like me. Anything there is will always involve me going down on my knees and cleaning up someone else's shit." Without warning he spluttered and coughed, he coughed so hard and violently that his eyes looked like they were about to pop out of his head. "I'm a fucking mess" he said while he wheezed and tried to suppress another phlegm filled splutter. I looked away from him and down to my feet while he tried to get his throat under control. Eventually he stopped choking and regained his composure. "Thanks again for coming", he said in a tone that made it clear that he wanted me to leave, "I appreciate it."

"That's ok" I said, "I hope that you're feeling better next time I see you." I didn't really know what I meant by the comment, it was meant as more of a friendly formality to make it easier for me to leave, but that's not how he took it.

"Thanks" he said, "but I doubt it. I don't have anything outside of this room. All I have is a bunch of books and that's it, and as much as I like books they aren't much comfort when I'm going to bed alone every night."

"What about your mother?" I asked, "You've got her."

"I know and I love her, but she's one of the reasons that I'm in here, she's great, but she's crazy. She practically force-fed me crap from the day that I was born because she wanted to make sure that no one else could ever love me. She made me leave school when I was 16 because she didn't want me to get good grades and go to university in case I became somebody and left her." He shook his head despairingly, I didn't think that any of what he said was true, but I didn't want to intrude on what was clearly an unresolved personal problem.

"I should go" I said quietly.

As I got up to leave he shot me a look of impatience, "what's wrong?" he asked. "Now that you've shown face is that you finished? Does that make you feel better about the hundreds of times you patronised me with all of that self-pitying crap about how shit your life is, your life with your perfect girlfriend, your flat in Highgate, your £30,000 salary, your dental insurance and your car?" I froze on the spot, I didn't want to stay, but the only reason I would have was to show that I wasn't just like the person he had described. "Please go ahead" he said.

"What's going to happen to you?" I asked with genuine concern.

"I don't know, for all I know my life might turn around tomorrow, or I might be straight back in here. Most likely I'll be more successful next time though, I don't want to make the same mistake twice." I looked into his dark calculating eyes; it was as if he was trying to read how unsettled I was. "You're not like me Floyd, all that separated me from this hospital bed was the £6.10 per hour that I got for cleaning up piss, and if I don't even have that anymore then I have nothing."

"I'm sorry" I said as I started to back off.

At the same time his mother came in from the hallway, she must have heard the raised voices and known that something was wrong. "Is everything ok?" she asked.

"Yes thanks, Floyd was just about to leave" he said icily.

I tried to give him a smile as I turned to leave, but he didn't notice. I didn't want to leave, but I felt that I had to. I wanted to run in and tell his mother what he had told me, but their relationship was obviously so far removed from normality that it was only likely to make things worse. I didn't know how much of what he said could be taken at face value, but as I left I was aware that it was likely to be the last time I would see him.

Chapter 29

My breakdown began with a sick and miserable cliché. It was a dreary Tuesday morning and I had just woken up with a head splitting, wine sponsored hangover. I felt absolutely terrible, and I left a sweaty outline behind me on my sheets as I pulled myself through to the bathroom to get ready for the day. I knew that the morning was being reserved for announcing staff cuts. They were meant to have been done the previous Friday, but because of Steven's antics they were still catching up a backlog, also, because Colin didn't work from the office on Tuesdays it meant that it would be safer for all concerned.

There were a lot of rumours going around about what really happened. Steven had tried to make himself look good by telling the key staff room gossips that he had been fired for punching Colin. This is obviously very different from if he had told them that he had actually punched Colin because he had been fired. At least four different people had asked me if it was true or not, and although I didn't like lying I saw no reason not to; it wasn't as if anyone was going to ask Colin for his side of the story.

I knew that the grapevine would be working against me that morning. I had spent the previous night at an impromptu leaving doo for Steven. It had been short notice so Janice hadn't been able to make it, but there were a good group of us. The night was nowhere near as much fun as our former Sunday night fares, and it was a lot more expensive. None of us felt comfortable in our jobs and all of us were stressed, which encouraged us to spend a stupidly high amount of our remaining wages on alcohol. The flashbacks in my head painted a messy picture; we had been thrown out of one bar and denied entry to another on the grounds that we were too drunk. Somewhere along the way Kenneth had urinated on a war memorial, one of our interns had been picked up by the police for vomiting in someone's front garden and I had got into a stupid argument with a bouncer at another pub, who did well to stop himself from breaking me in half.

I looked at the clock, I knew that it was about time for me to start getting ready, but it was painfully obvious that I was in no fit state to go to work. I was hung-over to the point that the idea of getting on a packed tube was too hellish to contemplate, and if I had tried to drive there in my condition then I would probably have lost my license. Even if I had been able to get there I wouldn't have been well enough to even pretend that I was working. Even more than that, in my heart I knew that I just couldn't face the prospect of another sterile and paranoia-filled day. Waiting to get fired was starting to feel almost as bad as I imagined it would be if they actually went through with it. It was one long boring stalemate situation, and it felt like the very most that I could hope for was another few days of treading water. It was self-defeating because I knew that if it wasn't yet my turn to go then it would be soon, but now that my two best friends were gone I didn't have anyone to pass the countdown with.

I didn't know what to do. I tried to drag myself to the sink, but I felt far too weak and tired, so instead I lowered myself down to the floor. I leaned against my bath and sat hunched forward on my cold and unwelcoming bathroom tiles. I wrapped my arms around my knees and my head tucked into my chest and desperately tried to think of a half decent excuse that I could use to avoid going to the office. I couldn't say that I was ill because that would almost certainly be interpreted as hung-over, and if word about the night before had got around then I would be in a lot of trouble. I had used the dentist and doctor excuses quite recently, so I couldn't use them. I also couldn't bring myself to say that a family tragedy had occurred because that seemed pretty sick. In the end I decided to say that I had got half way there and my car had broken down. I knew it was a terrible excuse but that didn't stop me from trying to convince an extremely sceptical secretary that I was going to be working from home. When she inevitably asked me why I didn't get on the tube like everyone else I couldn't think of a convincing answer, so instead I mumbled something incoherent about waiting for the postman and hung up.

A large part of me wanted to go back to bed and try to sleep though the pain, but there were builders doing something loud outside so I couldn't. The sounds from the drills and the shouting from the men on the scaffolding were too much for me. I couldn't think properly, they were shouting at each other and whatever it was that they were doing involved a lot of crashing and banging. The dulling sound of the drilling morphed into something more painful and I felt like my head was being taken over by noise when a police car passed by in the distance. Different visions of brutality and violence filled my mind and I thought about poor George alone in his hospital bed. As I considered his depressing fate I kept seeing flashes of barbarism and his self-harming amidst a backdrop of nothingness. The barbarism didn't stop at George and I found my mind focusing on the cracking sound that was caused by

Steven pounding on Colin's face. The crack sounded so satisfying, but I envisaged myself doing even more. I imagined myself beating his face in a flamboyantly OTT cartoon-like fashion. But the humour dried up when I got a vision of what I was doing to him. He appeared beaten and bloodied and he was looking directly at me through a mask of scarring and bruising.

It was all a mental image, but that didn't stop me from feeling like my small grey world was being turned upside down. I looked at what I had done to him and I wished that I could go back in time and undo everything. But I couldn't, and my feelings of self-disgust grew worse. The flashes of pain wouldn't leave me alone as my thoughts closed in on me and the wailing kept getting louder. I covered my ears with my hands, but that only trapped the sounds and visions and made it worse because I couldn't escape from them. A high pitched screech began from nowhere as I gasped and tears of regret ran down my burning hot cheeks. My heart began to beat faster and faster as the noise became even more piercing. In a state of panic I scrunched my hands into tight fists, and then I punched myself hard in the side of the skull. The impact nullified the noise a little, so I did it again and again, but it wouldn't fully stop until I had done myself some serious damage.

Finally everything stopped. Calm descended from above and I waited for my heart to stop beating at 1000mph before I forced myself to stand up and look in the mirror. I looked like I had been completely battered. I felt physically sick as I coughed up a lump of blood that was so thick and red that it didn't look real. I opened a tube of jaw numbing painkillers and washed down a handful of them with a bitter mouthful of menthol flavoured Listerine. Then I splashed some cold water onto my face and tried to doctor what was left of my looks.

I sat on my toilet and used some cotton wool to pad my self-inflicted wounds, and then I phoned Steven. I knew that he probably wasn't going to want to hear any of it, but he was probably the only person that I could think of who would still give a shit about me now that Janice was gone. "Floyd, you need to go to work", he said through his hangover. "Everyone will be talking about last night, and from what I remember of it you were being a complete dick." I tried to explain that I was ill but it was no use. "Just go in" he said, "or otherwise you'll end up unemployed like me."

I went through to the kitchen to pour a glass of water, and then I found myself looking to my mail for support. All that I could find were bills, circulars, junk, adverts and threats of future repossession notices. I didn't want to think about any of those things, so I put them to one side and scanned the worktop for anything that could distract me. On the other side of the room I saw a half empty bottle of red wine that was tempting me to stay. But the knives on the block next to my chopping boards were the wrong way up and they kept making me think of George's wrist as it lay hidden below a pile of life prolonging cables and bad memories. I focused on their cold metal tips and imagined the damage that they could do to his soft tender skin. I felt a tight wrench in my throat as I finished my water in one long sip and stepped out of the room.

Although the flat was empty it also felt incredibly constraining and stuffy. It was so enclosed, and it felt much smaller than usual. I had a cold sweat running down my back as I looked through my windows and onto the bleak streets and the bland gray skyline that lay beyond. The only person I could think of, and at that moment the only person that I genuinely wanted to speak to, was Penelope. I hadn't thought about her all that much lately, but at that moment I felt an urgent desire to just sit down with her and talk to her. I went through to the phone in my bedroom and tried to call her mobile, but then I remembered that it was her dad who had it so I hung up before it could begin ringing.

I knew that I had to get out of London. I smoked a cigarette and put a rough plan together in my head. I decided that I was going to go down to Brighton to find her and talk to her, and I decided that when I found her I would get down on my knees and beg for her forgiveness.

I didn't know how long I would need, so I had a shower and packed a few of my most important things. I packed a change of clothes, my wallet, my keys, my Oyster Card and my Blackberry. My Blackberry had been vibrating continuously all morning, and a mix of work related emails and spam from Viagra companies and 'Ugandan Kings' had taken over my inbox. Among them was an invitation for a meeting with Sophie that afternoon, as I read the description I knew that it could only be bad news.

I double-locked the door behind me and went to the station. My head felt a lot better, but I still looked rough. As I sat on the train I thought about everything. The last few months played through in my head like some kind of evil montage. I could see my descent up close and I felt so helpless. I didn't know what I was going to do and I didn't even know where I was going to stay. I didn't have any game plan or any reason to believe that it would work, but I didn't have much to lose.

Chapter 30

Brighton was nothing like I had imagined. I had grown up with the image of it as a big, camp, happy town where panto-dames and local characters sat on the beach all day drinking cocktails and eating chips. Unfortunately it was nothing of the sort. My first experiences of the city were of a homeless man calling me a 'toffee nosed wanker' when I walked past him, and a group of school children scrawling homophobic graffiti outside the train station. I was somewhat disillusioned as I made my way to the beach and found out that it was just as dreary and grey as anywhere else in England.

I had found out her work address by Googling her name and the word Brighton repeatedly until something came up. After some searching I found that she had a new Linkedin profile which said that she was working for a small PR firm that specialised in travel and tourism. I didn't have anywhere else to go, so I waited on a bench outside her office for two hours and tried to think about what I was going to say. In my most optimistic versions of events I wouldn't have to say anything, she would just be so unspeakably happy to see me that she would run over and hug me, then we would go back to her house, pack her stuff, head to London and pretend that nothing had ever happened.

When I eventually saw her she looked stunning; she was slender, sexy and dressed in a black power suit that ensured she looked every bit the part of a corporate high flyer. I saw her stepping out of the front door, at first she didn't notice me, but when she did it became very obvious that she didn't want to forgive and forget.

She stopped walking, and then she shook her head and looked at me with a mixture of shock, surprise and contempt. An uneasy silence hung in the air. I got up from the bench and stepped forward to break it, but I didn't have the time to form any words. "I'm in a rush" she said, as she looked down to her feet and went back inside.

I was too taken aback to call after her, so I froze as she walked away from me and back into her office. At first I stood with my jaw dropped, and then I went back to the bench and tried to figure everything out all over again. I didn't know what to do; I had no desire to spend another second in Brighton, but I also couldn't face the prospect of going back to London and trying to enthuse myself about a job that I was about to lose and a life that I didn't really care much about.

I knew that I couldn't hang around outside for much longer, but I didn't want to go home without getting a final answer, so I went to a beachside bar and pieced together a radical plan for one last high risk roll of the dice.

***

I had a self-destructive spring in my step as I returned to her office at 5.30 with a massive bouquet of flowers and a box of heart shaped chocolates. I smiled confidently, I knew that this would either be the last time I ever saw her or the start of a whole new era in our relationship. As she stepped out she forced herself to smile, she had obviously been expecting me.

"Penelope" I began, "I come here as a sorry shell of my former self, I am broken and I am tired. I am so sorry to be causing such a public scene, but over the last few months I have been to hell and back. And now I know that it's because I still love you, and I have never been so sure of anything in my life."

"Oh dear god" she mumbled to herself.

I froze in fear as I realised that her reaction was nothing like the one that I wanted and everything like the one that I dreaded. I had hoped that with an afternoon of thinking about me she would remember all of the good times that I had clearly forgotten about when I had dumped her. I had hoped that she would have missed me so much that she would be jumping at the chance to get back together. But she wasn't, so there I was standing in a busy Brighton street with flowers, chocolates and a girl who was looking at me with such indifference that I was questioning whether or not even I knew what I was doing.

"Penelope" I said again as I stepped forward, "I really wish that I could undo everything from the last couple of months and be the Floyd who you fell in love with." I grinned a big toothy grin, but she rolled her eyes and visibly cringed at the thought that she could ever have been in love with me.

"Floyd, please don't do this. It's embarrassing and there are people everywhere. My colleagues will all be watching from the windows, you're causing a scene."

"You haven't seen anything yet" I said defiantly. "Penelope, I want you to come back to London and move in with me again." There was a silence, "But this time I want it to be different."

BOOM!

I could see a look of horror forming in her eyes as I put the flowers and chocolates to one side and got down on one knee. If I was going to be rejected then at least I was going to go whole hog. I didn't actually have a ring but my voice held firm as I dug my hole even deeper. "Penelope, I know that this must be unexpected, but I want you back, and nothing would make me happier than for you to say that you will be my wife."

Silence.

She looked over her shoulders to make sure no-one was watching before she came closer. "Why are you doing this?"

"Because if I don't then I know that you'll turn around and walk away and then I'll never have the chance to make it up to you."

"So let me get it straight, this is your attempt to apologise to me?"

"Yes" I said firmly and unapologetically.

"And you honestly thought that asking me to marry you would be the best way to say sorry?"

"Yes. I know that this will sound totally ridiculous, but I don't want to leave any questions unanswered. I don't have anything to lose, and if I had just gone back to London without making a spectacle then I would have always wondered what you would have said."

"Floyd, please stop it" she said sternly, "of course I am not going to marry you."

"Please at least think about coming back with me."

"Floyd, even if I wanted to, which I don't, then I couldn't. I have a new life and a new career now."

"But London has lots of PR firms and all of your friends are there."

She sighed. "I also have a new boyfriend" she said.

BOOM! My plans hadn't just fallen apart, they had been totally obliterated.

"You do?" I asked timidly.

"Yes" she said, "His name is Chris and he'll be here any minute. Besides, even if I didn't then I still wouldn't want to go back. I have never been happier than I was on the day that I realised I don't need you anymore. I was so angry when you left me. You had forced me out of a mess of your making, and at first I wanted to get back at you. But then one day I stopped being angry and I realised that I was never going to feel that way about you again."

"So is this it all over for good?"

"Yes."

"Is there really nothing at all that I can say or do?" I asked pathetically.

"There is one thing" she said.

"What's that?"

"Go home."

Chapter 31

I drank all night. I had just been totally humiliated so I had no reason not to. I don't remember what I was drinking; I don't even know who I was drinking with and I have no idea what happened throughout significant periods of the night. I know that I was in a few different places because I can remember flashing lights and I have vague recollections of pounding disco music and a bright room with glitter-balls and possibly strippers, but none of it adds up to anything meaningful or substantial. I remember dancing into the early hours of the morning with a group of men in fancy dress who could have been on a stag night. I can also remember myself falling over in the street a few times and I can remember throwing up after eating a greasy kebab by the pier.

It must have been really late because fat Elvis impersonators and drag queens were the only other people who were still out when I eventually found a place to stay. I searched for a while until I found a nice little hostel that was willing to take me in. I leeringly spoke to the receptionist and negotiated a price for the day, and then with some assistance I managed to maneuver my way up three flights of stairs and into a big dark bedroom.

I was woken up a few hours later by an angry maid. I apologised for the mess and literally rolled out of bed so that she could clean it. The light in the hallway was overpowering, it was like the poisonous cherry on top of an utterly horrible cake. I didn't feel at all clean and I was still in the same shirt, trousers and socks that I had been wearing the night before. I was pretty ashamed, but I was far too tired, and drunk, to suffer the full level of humiliation that was rightfully mine. I'm sure lots of people must have walked past but I wasn't awake enough to notice any of them.

***

When I was allowed back in I took off my dirty clothes and threw myself back on to bed, where I slept for the best part of the afternoon. I don't think that I dreamt about anything, it was more like a blackout. When I woke up I felt even worse than I had before. I couldn't believe that I had found myself in such a pathetic position. I cried that afternoon, so much anger, frustration and anxiety had been building up for a long time and I needed to release it in the most self-pitying and futile way possible. How could I end up like this? I had been born with every social advantage possible. As I felt at the bruising all over my face and looked to the vomit stains on my shoes I couldn't help feeling that things like that weren't meant to happen to people like me.

When I eventually got out of the bed I put on my trousers and shirt again, I had no idea where I could have put the bag of clean clothes that I had brought with me. I wanted to check the time so I turned to find my Blackberry, but it was gone. I padded down all of my pockets but it was nowhere. I couldn't find my wallet either, then I felt one of those moments of total clarity, I realised that I was screwed.

***

Once I was dressed I went down to the reception and tried to explain everything to a mousey young girl who was obviously trying to avoid making any eye contact with me. The other customers had looked slightly scared as I had made my way downstairs, which didn't do anything to alleviate either her concerns or my shame. The manager soon came to the desk. He asked me to follow him and then he took me into his office. He wasn't very sympathetic, but what could I say? I didn't have any money, and I had no idea what had happened to any of my things. For all I knew they could be anywhere. Regardless of where they were I wasn't able to pay. I had a few coins in my pocket, but they weren't even enough to pay for a coffee let alone my room.

***

I was made to spend the night in a police cell, which wasn't actually as bad as it could have been. Having said that, I doubt that there are many things that could be as embarrassing as when I was dragged out of the building wearing handcuffs. There wasn't a lot of small talk, although they went through the usual spiel and read me my rights. The cell itself was small, harsh and lonely, but at least I could let myself sober up and rest for a while. The police had actually been generally quite decent about everything. They must have seen far worse people than me and I think that they pitied me more than anything else. They gave me my first proper meal in days and let me take a shower. As I lay on the tough mattress I counted the tiles on the roof and reflected on how badly my plan for reunification had gone.

When they let me out I went back to the hostel and tried to apologise to the receptionist, but she didn't want to speak to me. I managed to talk to the lost property people but they said no-one had handed anything in. When I left I took a walk into the city centre and went to Carphone Warehouse so that I could cancel my phone contract. I also visited a local branch of my bank and they were able to cancel my card and let me take out enough money to get back to London.

***

Before I left I took a short walk down by the sea. The air was so much fresher than what I was used to. It wasn't exactly the Promised Land but it seemed like somewhere that I could be happy. Everywhere I looked I saw loved up young couples pairing off hand in hand, they were enjoying the outdoors and each other's company. I felt a pang of jealousy. I had skipped that whole section of growing up by getting into a relationship at a time when what I probably needed was the usual diet of teenage fumbling and character building heartbreak.

I smoked a cigarette on the edge of the pier and watched some kids swimming out to nowhere in particular. They looked hopeful and optimistic, and it occurred to me that they might grow up to be the ones who would push themselves into achieving something while people like me, and the rest of Generation Debt, wallowed in our collective misery. Could it be that we only stopped dreaming because everyone else around us did? Maybe one of the reasons that we all feel so helpless is because everyone around us does. I kept watching them until they turned into little pink specks in the distance.

***

When I got back I had to visit Steven to get his spare keys for my house. He seemed pretty miserable and down, but I didn't bother sticking around for any chat as I just wanted to get to bed. When I managed to get home I found the inevitable voicemail from Sophie. "Floyd, I don't know where you are but you certainly aren't at work. I have called your mobile, I have called your home, and I have even called your doctor. I'm assuming that you're not going to be in today and so you won't be surprised to know that unless you're found dead in a ditch somewhere then you're fired. Thank you." It was painful to hear, but it wasn't unexpected.

I shrugged it off and poured some tea, lit a cigarette, cast aside an unloved, crisis induced, Dr Dre CD and put on my favourite Morrissey album. As his songs of regret filled the air I managed to crack a smile at their familiarity. All things considered I felt strangely calm and upbeat for someone who had been rejected by his only proper girlfriend to date, lost all of his stuff on a night out, spent another night in jail and then arrived home to discover that he had just been fired during the worst recession in a generation.

As for how I lost my house, that's a much simpler and even more humbling story.

Now that I was unemployed there was no way that I could afford the rent on a nice one bedroom flat in north London, I could barely even afford it when I was working. It was almost exactly seven years to the day since I had originally moved out, but now I had no choice other than to pack my stuff and head back to my parents' house.

Chapter 32

Postscript

Things have moved on over the last few months, but some things are still the same. The City is still in ruins and the company itself is deeper in the red than ever. With all of the sickening greed there have been ever-growing protests from the usual suspects, and for all but the privileged few it's been a terrible time to work in finance. The government have responded to the protests with a mixture of heavy handed policing and tax breaks to help the super rich 'rebuild' our country. The super rich and their FTSE 100 friends have responded in the same way that they always do, by taking the money and running, in some cases literally. Globalisation has reared its multinational head and now tens of thousands of skilled jobs like mine are being outsourced to India and South East Asia.

There's no obvious end in sight. The troubles are only escalating as greater unemployment means even greater resentment and even greater social breakdown. I'm still incredibly angry about the fact that my grandmother, who was a part of the generation who defeated Hitler, died alone and scared. For the last few years of her life she had been a recluse. Every time she had gone outside she had found something new to be afraid of. If it wasn't kids in hoods smashing up phone boxes then it was an army of skin heads and their beastly dogs. She felt that her whole generation were betrayed so that we could all live with the grim consequences of someone else's post war dream; a dream that has comprised of excesses for the few and insecurity for the masses.

It's to this backdrop that I've come to realise how much better I am for being out of the monetary system's depressing bubble. Whenever I watch the news I find myself cheering for the protesters. I keep thinking about rediscovering the same fighting spirit as I had once dreamt of as a teenager and joining them on the picket lines and the barricades. These feelings of radicalism are counterbalanced by a combination of my natural cowardice and the fact that we're entering winter so it's cold outside. The fact that I would rather be warm than overthrowing the government suggests that my disengagement is pretty puerile and my revolutionary feelings are only skin-deep.

***

Steven kept a low profile for a while, but now he's found a new job in the city and he's back to his bad old ways of spending loosely and living off false credit. There's a new sense of fragility about him as he's feeling more insecure in his job with every passing day and he's broken off his friendship with Brogan. He said that she came round to see him one night when he was between jobs and he was feeling particularly miserable. He had never seen her before, but when he did she looked so young and innocent, and that made him feel bad about the fact she was there. To make matters worse she hit on him, at least that's what he says. He told me that he went to the kitchen to get them something to drink and when he got back she had taken her top off and asked him if he wanted to have sex with her. He says that he told her to put her clothes back on and asked her to leave. He said that they tried to stay friends afterwards, but it didn't work. The whole reason that he liked her was because he didn't know her and he could talk to her and know that she wouldn't judge him, but now that he's met it's changed everything.

It's because I'm out in the countryside that I don't see very much of him, but when I do he's far quieter and more subdued. In a rare candid moment he's admitted to me that he's recently been feeling very lonely. I believe him and I can understand how he feels. I also can't help feeling that since he lost his job he's lost a part of what made him the Steven who I knew. I also feel that this insecure and slightly socially awkward version of him is probably the person that he always was beneath all of his bullshit and his bravado.

Sophie's still at the company, but the last few weeks at work, and the hatred that comes with axing hundreds of jobs, have been a major wake up call for her. She's recently been all-over the trade press in an effort to resurrect her image and rationalise all of the bad things that she's done. We haven't properly spoken since she fired me. She sent me an email shortly afterwards to ask how I was doing, but I didn't bother to get back to her. It's a lot easier for her to try and be nice about things now that Colin has finally gone. The stress of everything became too much and he had a breakdown. Now he's living off a golden parachute and an advanced payment for his memoirs; which he's writing from the safe sanctuary of one of those exclusive gated communities where rich businessmen go to die.

Sadly he's not the only one who's gone. George stayed true to his word and killed himself almost as soon as he was out of hospital. This time he was taking no chances and he came up with a horrible plan to make sure that he would succeed.

He had a couple of drinks for Dutch-courage and then he jumped over the edge of a bridge that overlooked the M25 and landed headfirst on top of a moving vehicle. His death was barely mentioned in the media, I only found out because I was worried about him so I kept an eye on the announcements page of the local paper. I had a horrible feeling of regret as I went to his funeral, I kept thinking about what I could have done. It was a very small service and there were only a few of us there. His mother gave me the kind of soft familiar smile that said that she wanted to talk to me. I didn't feel like I could go to the wake, it would have made it seem even more real and like even more of a tragic waste of life. When I got home I sent her a card.

As for Penelope, I feel like I'm finally over her. It may have taken me two other women, a breakdown and a botched proposal, but I feel like I've turned a corner. Being rejected by her was almost liberating because it drew a line under everything once and for all. Now I feel like I'm in a better position to take on whatever lies ahead. I don't have any money so I don't need to worry about losing it and my ego has taken far too much off a battering for me to be smug about myself.

I can still see an alternative version of events in which we had persevered with it all and stayed together. We would probably have bobbed along quite nicely and eventually tied the knot. Then we would have enjoyed a mediocre marriage, during which we both have wondered about what could have been with someone else. We could have settled down, grown old together and grown apart, and then we could have tried to cement our relationship with children so that we were unable to escape.

The alternative reality that I can envisage with Venus feels like more of a loss. I can imagine us dating, I can imagine us having passionate sex and I can imagine us watching the sun going down from that same old bench we carved our names into. We could have turned our lives into the sort of fairytale romance where every experience would have been golden and every day would have been a blessing. I'm not saying that there wouldn't have been problems, but it would have been nice to see where it would have lead. There will never be a time when I don't regret what I did to her. I know that she's not forgiven me yet because I've tried calling and emailing her but she's never got back to me. With Penelope and Venus having all but erased me from their lives it's only a matter of time before Sophie gets around to doing the same thing, and then it'll be like my love rectangle never existed.

***

I visited Janice a few days ago. She's doing the marketing and accounts for April's fair-trade clothing company, it's not going to wipe out global poverty but it will help some people to live better lives and it keeps her smiling. Her new house is really nice, she's become an archetypal country girl and she only ever goes into the city if it's really urgent. She's kept her subscription to the Economist though, so some old habits die hard.

She has a new boyfriend too. They met at the local pub, his name's John and he's a fireman, which is just too wonderfully clichéd to be true. He lives in a little thatched cottage next to a lake and they spend their weekends doing all sorts of quirky and quaint countryside things like horse riding, picking mushrooms and making soup.

When I was up there we talked for hours, we drank two bottles of wine and fell asleep together on her couch. I told her about Sophie, at first I thought that she would be really mad but she barely even cared. "None of that stuff even matters anymore" she said calmly. "I always kind of suspected it anyway, but it's irrelevant because it was Sophie, so it can't possibly have meant anything."

***

There have been so many times that I've thought I could do with a wish, or at least some good fortune. The truth is that I've had it all along. The problems that I've had have almost all been of my own making, but thankfully I've had a couple of really good friends to help me every step of the way. Ultimately I believe that we become the people who we are because of the experiences that we have and the people that we share them with, and I didn't like the person who I had let myself become. I was able to work through my problems, but that was only because of the good people around me. Tragically George was someone who never had any of my good circumstances or any good friends, and so there was no-one to help him when he needed it the most. The pain he must have felt when he jumped from that bridge is something I can't even begin to imagine, but it doesn't feel like a suicide, it feels like he was another innocent victim of a cold harsh system that had chewed him up and fucked him up to the point of self-destruction.

In contrast, none of my problems were so big, none of them were inevitable and they could all have easily been solved by talking. If only I had taken the time to talk to Penelope then we wouldn't have ended up like we did. I'm not saying that we would have sorted everything out, but it's unlikely that I would have trailed down to Brighton in a horrific state and then spent the night in a cell. Had I just spoken to Sophie and made sure that we were on the same page from the outset of our 'relationship' then I could have saved her a lot of heartache and possibly my job. When I think of Venus I think about all of the missed opportunities and about how much I let myself rush into everything. There was no way that I was ready for it, so why couldn't I be candid with her? In all of these cases there were really compelling reasons to be honest, so I have no idea why I wasn't. I also cringe a little when I think about the numerous times I've repressed those potentially awkward conversations with my friends or my parents. Why can't I bring myself to talk to Steven about the scars on his arms, or finally talk to my dad about what his affairs did to our family? I don't know why it has taken me so long to realise that there is no shame in showing your vulnerabilities, what is it that we all get so scared of?

It seems to me that lies and repression only compound our problems, because as much as we try we can never get rid of them. I fantasise about an alternative reality in which I had been honest and transparent in everything I did. Just imagine if we all had the conversations that we were putting off, imagine if all human relationships were devoured by a tidal wave of honesty, what if we all finally said what was on our minds? I can't imagine that things would go any worse

A few days ago I was sitting in a cafe and two elderly women came in with their carer. As he went to the counter to order tea the two women sat opposite each other at the table next to mine. One of them had a stick which she propped up beside her as she leaned forward to talk to her friend, who was much smaller than her, and was sitting in a wheelchair, she looked worried and tired. The woman with the stick gently offered her hand, which her friend took, and seemed instantly less anxious. She quietly reassured her that she didn't need to worry.

One thing I am sure of is that if wealth were measured by the friends that we keep then I would be a millionaire many times over. Janice, Steven and I have been through so much together, and hopefully there will be far more to come. Because our age is one of nihilism, consumerism and fatalism, and because the people that we care about are so few and far between, then I will never stop thinking about them. As long as London is burning and the world is still collapsing all around us then our bonds are the only things that we have left.

***

Now that I'm living with my parents I have endless views of fields and trees. I'm starting to appreciate them a bit more as opposed to seeing them as a horrible preview of a post apocalyptic world. We've become a lot closer too. I've even found the courage to start speaking to my dad about everything that's happened. I told him about how much I had hated turning 25 and how I had tried to blame that for everything that followed. At first he laughed, and then he dismissed it all with one swift shake of his head and said something that was both comforting in its remoteness and chilling in its simplicity; "25 is nothing, just wait until you reach 50."